FROZEN WORLD

FROZEN WORLD

Scott M. Baker

Also by Scott M. Baker

Anthologies

Cruise of the Living Dead and other Stories

Incident on Ironstone Lane and Other Horror Stories

Crossroads in the Dark V: Beyond the Borders (under the name Josh Matthews)

Rejected for Content (under the name Matthew Arkham)

Roots of a Beating Heart

The Zombie Road Fan Fiction Collection

The Collector

A Schattenseite Book

Frozen World

By Scott M. Baker.
Copyright © 2021. All Rights Reserved.
Print Edition
ISBN-13: 978-1-7365915-1-2

Cover Art © Warren Design

To my father.

CHAPTER ONE

THE NOON SUN shone down on the compacted snow that stretched in every direction as far as the horizon. Occasionally, the flat surface was interrupted by a mound of snow created by the wind and frozen in place by the bitter cold. Ice crystals reflected the light, so the ground for miles around appeared to sparkle. Gusts of wind from the north, accelerated by the flat and barren landscape, gathered up the few loose flakes, churning them into white eddies that coasted along the landscape, almost as if an artist had lightly dabbed his paintbrush across the canvas. It would have been a beautiful scene if those inside the Hagglund tracked vehicle did not have to wear dark sunglasses to dim the intensity of the glare and prevent snow blindness.

A lot of the newbies enjoyed being assigned to the EDF, the Exterior Defense Force. They found Above Earth fascinating, filled with wonder and beauty, and a welcome break from the monotony of living in "the bunker." Colonel Mark Denning, the commander of the EDF, knew otherwise. Seated in the passenger seat of the Hagglund, he realized the view in front of him concealed a terrible lie. However beautiful it may seem, the picturesque landscape masked the dangerous reality that the outside world held dangers nobody underground could comprehend. Those who never traveled to the surface were ignorant of them, like how unpredictable the terrain could be, with deep, snow-covered fissures that could swallow the unsuspecting into icy tombs. How easily one could become disoriented and lost in this never-ending, monotonous terrain, which would be a death sentence. How quickly the cold could drain the life from one's body. How uncompromising this environment could be, and how fragile existence was in it.

Denning had worked in this environment for thirteen years of his own volition. Upper Earth was his mistress, a mistress he loved and feared at the same time. Sure, it had nearly killed him on almost a dozen occasions, but he kept coming back. Those under his command misread his reasoning for staying with the EDF. Some considered him a thrill-seeker. Others believed he needed to confront his fears. A few whispered amongst themselves that he had a death wish. They were all wrong. Denning stayed with the EDF because of the prestige. In an era where conformity and status were the norms, he thrived on being different. The histories mentioned that in the time before the Great Freeze, only fifty-three hundred people had ever made it to the top of Mount Everest, the highest mountain in the Old World. Less than four thousand people in the USC had ever been topside. It made him unique.

Days such as this were the downside to the rush. First Shift had called in to notify him they had discovered Team Four, which had been missing since last night.

Kenneth, the driver, had been following the tracks left by the three Hagglunds already at the scene. As they circled a snowdrift, the vehicles came into view. The three-person crews stayed inside their vehicles rather than expose themselves to the elements. Even from this distance, Denning noticed the three bodies lying sprawled out across the snow. As they approached, Third Captain Buddy Haskell, the First Shift Commanding Officer, climbed out of the closest vehicle and came over to greet him.

Denning opened the passenger door. Despite the heavy thermal suit, the icy blast of air sliced through his body, causing him to wince. As he made his way over to Haskell, the rest of the EDF team formed a protective circle around the group, except for one soldier who wandered over to the bodies.

Haskell saluted. "I hate to bring you out here so early in the morning."

"Especially for something like this." The only part of this job Denning hated involved the death of team members. "What do you have?"

"First Shift found Team Four this morning." Haskell waved for his CO to follow. They headed for the Hagglund that sat away from the others, its doors open. "The scene is exactly as Sergeant Whitaker found it."

Denning paused and scanned the interior of the vehicle. Somebody had stripped it of anything not bolted down, mostly the food, water, extra clothing, and medical supplies each unit took with them on their shift. Something had vandalized the console, breaking the glass dials, ripping off the switches, and tearing out the wiring. Claw-like scratches stretched across the seats, gouging the upholstery.

"The same thing happened to the engine," said Haskell. "Someone ripped out the wires and belts."

"And this is how you found it?"

"Yes, sir. We didn't even close the doors."

"What about the crew?"

"They're over here." Haskell led the way to where three naked bodies lay side by side in the snow. Terrance lay on his back, his abdomen torn open and half of his intestines and organs missing, with the other half spread around the body resting on a frozen pool of blood. Unger lay face down, the flesh and muscles from his back and buttocks having been gorged on. Denning recognized him only by the EDF emblem tattooed on his left arm. The third body, belonging to a young newbie whose name he had not yet memorized, rested on her right side. Every ounce of flesh and muscle on her exposed side, from her ankles to her head, had been torn off and devoured. Her left arm was missing below the shoulder. Each had been stripped naked, but none of their clothes, gear, or weapons had been left behind. A small hole half an inch across burrowed through the back of their skulls, the wounds frozen over.

Denning studied the bodies. "Did you find their uniforms?"

Haskell shook his head. "Everything is gone, even their ID cards."

"And their weapons?"

"Same."

"Shit," Denning mumbled.

He crouched by Unger and attempted to roll him over. The head would not move. A large, crimson ice patch had formed beneath his face, the blood having cemented the skin to the ice. The colonel tried again but stopped when he realized doing so would only peel the dead man's skin from his muscles. Unger had suffered enough indignity already. Two splotches of blood lay near Terrance and the newbie. He examined their bodies again. The tops of their heads were shattered.

Haskell answered the question he knew would be asked. "It looks like someone shot them in the back of the head after stripping them naked. Quick, clean deaths. They never felt the polar bears feed off them."

"Any footprints leading out of the area?"

"Just those from the bears." Haskell pointed to the tracks leading north. "Whoever killed them knew what they were doing."

"Fuck." Denning took a few steps away from the scene and stared out across the landscape. Like his predecessors, he knew such a possibility existed. The more time that had elapsed since the Great Freeze, the lesser the chances had become. But the possibility, however minimal, always remained. Now it had become a reality. The only uncertainty involved what would play out next.

Heading back to his Hagglund, Denning motioned for Haskell to follow. "The official story is that Team Four's vehicle lost power and the crew died of exposure. Make sure everyone here knows that if anyone says otherwise, they'll all be doing double shifts out here for the rest of their tours."

"Roger that. What should I do about the remains?"

"I'll send a retrieval vehicle out later today to bring the tractor and the bodies back to base. We'll announce their deaths tomorrow and give them a proper burial with full honors. They deserve it." Denning reached his tractor, opened the door, and climbed inside. "As for your teams, continue with the daily routine. Just warn them to be extra cautious. We don't know if the danger is still in the area. If they encounter any polar bears, kill them on sight."

"Yes, sir. Are you heading back?"

"I have to inform the Governor we made first contact."

CHAPTER TWO

MAYA WOKE UP with a happiness she had not felt in a while. And not only because Devon's hard-on pressed against her butt cheeks. They had been together for over a year now. She loved Devon Williams and, even though he never spoke the words, she knew he felt the same way about her.

Maya could barely contain her excitement. Today she would be sworn in as a cadet in the Exterior Defense Force, the most prestigious unit in Underground Survival Center 7, second only to the government elite. Her days cleaning tables and washing dishes were behind her forever.

Usually, only those on Rings B and C were allowed into the EDF or the IDF, the Interior Defense Force. Being born and raised on Ring D, where the workers resided, would have precluded her from such an honor. After turning twenty-one, Maya believed she would be considered too old to join. However, after they began dating, Devon had pulled some strings, informing Colonel Denning she would be a valuable recruit. The colonel called in a few favors and got her enrolled despite her age. Not only would this position provide her with an opportunity to get out of the bunker and see Above Earth, but the benefits that came with the job were excellent. After ten years with the EDF, she would transfer over to the IDF, perhaps doing a tour on the Governor's security detail. After twenty years with the IDF, she could retire with honors and choose a job working in Ring A. She would also be granted living quarters in Ring C, which were far superior to those she currently lived in.

The world lay at her feet, and Maya knew the perfect way to start such a day as well as thank the man who made it all possible.

Devon spooned Maya, his still erect manhood against her. She rolled him onto his back and straddled him. Maya slid Devon inside of her, moaning as his size filled her. She began slowly riding him.

Devon opened his eyes, a huge smile on his face. "I hope this isn't a dream."

"It's my way of saying thank you for getting me this job. Just enjoy it."

He did. Maya knew how to make her man happy. She ground against him and twisted her buttocks until he began breathing heavily. A minute later, he arched his hips to meet her thrusts and finished inside of her. She didn't mind not getting off herself. When finished, she leaned over and kissed him, collapsing on his chest.

"Did you enjoy that?" she purred.

"It was perfect. Like you." Devon wrapped his arms around her, one hand stroking her auburn hair.

"You can finish me off tonight."

"Did you forget that you'll be spending the next eight weeks in the barracks with the other recruits?"

Shit, she had forgotten about that.

"Even if you could come back here, you'll be too tired after your first day with the EDF."

"How bad is boot camp going to be?"

"They're going to be tough on you. But since you've worked in Ring E for so long, it won't be as bad for you as it will for the other recruits."

"They'll go easy on me because of you," Maya joked.

Devon chuckled. "Don't count on it. If anything, they'll be tougher with you to show there's no favoritism."

"Do you think I'm up to it?" she asked with all seriousness.

"I wouldn't have recommended you if I thought you

weren't."

Maya kissed him on his chest.

"As much as I would like to stay here with you, I have to meet the Governor early and prepare for the swearing-in ceremony." Devon gently rolled Maya to her side of the bed and climbed out. He stepped over to the room's control console.

Damn, he looked good naked.

"What view do you want?"

"Can you call up an outside view?"

"Sure." Devon punched a command into the console. A few seconds later, the curtains in front of him parted. "There you go. I'm going to take a shower."

As Devon went into the bathroom, Maya swung out of bed and made her way to the window.

Each room on Rings A through D had its own window. Normally, the view would look out on the rock walls surrounding each ring of the underground community. The developers realized that would get tiresome quickly, so they installed video screens in front of the windows. A person could choose from over a hundred different images of life from the Old World, from tropical settings, beach scenes, mountains, green plains, or seventy-five views of old cities like Paris and Moscow long since buried under tons of ice and snow. Maya enjoyed the scenic videos. Born and raised in USC7, she had never seen any of the places downloaded, so they meant nothing to her.

She watched the video that showed the area directly above them, the only one shown in real-time. All the others were recorded from earlier days. Wind gusted by the mounds, blowing off loose snow that spiraled across the frozen landscape.

The video screen slowly grew brighter. The developers also realized that having one constant level of light would throw off the citizens' circadian rhythms, making adjusting to their new environment much more challenging. They fixed that problem by timing the lighting fixtures in the public sectors of the bunker and the video screens to match the cycles on Above Earth. They would increase early in the morning and decrease as the day wore on. At night, the screens would show the scenes and landscapes in the moonlight while the corridor lighting would dim. Rumor had it that the first occupants of USC7 found it irritating but, over time, it became the norm. Those born here accepted the cycles as part of life.

Devon came out of the bathroom. Maya watched him as he dressed. As much as she enjoyed seeing him naked, Devon cut a dashing figure in his uniform. The navy-blue slacks hid his muscular leg muscles, but the light blue shirt fit nicely around his tight chest and broad shoulders, leaving little to the imagination. Today he wore a navy-blue tie for the swearing-in ceremony and an accompanying dress jacket. Only the tan work boots that everyone wore distracted from his appearance. Devon was a ton of handsome stuffed into a six-foot body. She wished he didn't have to leave right this minute.

He adjusted his uniform in the mirror then put on his dress cap, covering his close-cut dark hair.

"You better hurry and get ready," he said, turning from the mirror. "The last thing a recruit wants to do is be late for their first day."

"Sheesh, bossing me around already."

Devon smiled. On his way out, he stopped to kiss Maya.

"I'm so proud of you. See you at the ceremony."

When he left, Maya rushed into the bathroom and took her shower.

CHAPTER THREE

MAYA RUSHED THROUGH the corridors of USC7, trying to make it to the Ceremony Hall in time. She had spent more time than she had anticipated choosing an outfit for the occasion from the minimal amount of clothes she owned. Now she raced against the clock, knowing that if she arrived late, Devon would have to chew her out, not because he wanted to but because he needed to treat her like any other recruit as an officer of the EDF. Usually, this would not be a problem. Maya knew her way around the outer layers of the structure but had never visited Rings A and B.

USC7 was a large underground structure built for maximum efficiency. Devon told her its design had been based on the Pentagon, a military building quite famous in the Old World. He said the Pentagon used to be as wide as the Empire State Building or a container cargo ship, neither reference having any significance to her. USC7 measured forty times larger, a city of two million inhabitants constructed a thousand feet below Above Earth.

The basic design consisted of a five-sided structure with ten floors for living and working spaces as well as four sub-basements. All fourteen levels consisted of five rings connected by eight equidistant corridors running from the outer ring to the center. The outer ring, Ring E, held the manufacturing and maintenance sectors. Ninety percent of the population worked here or in the sub-basements producing the necessary daily supplies needed to survive. Ring D contained living quarters for the workers, all of whom worked in Ring E or the sub-basements. Living quarters there consisted of six single people to a small room or one small room for families. Ring C housed the managers, most of whom ran operations in Ring E and the sub-basements, and EDF/IDF personnel. The latter each received a private room, like Devon. Ring B contained the living quarters for central government officials and the eight mayors of USC7. The Governor and her staff received four-room apartments, and the mayors and their staff got three and two-room apartments, respectively. When someone was voted out during elections, they would return to Ring C and the new leaders would take over their apartments. Ring A, the inner ring and therefore the smallest, had been reserved for government offices, ceremonial suites, and barracks and training facilities for the EDF/IDF cadets. The unseemly aspects of city life were cosigned to the basement—garbage collection; sewage treatment and disposal to a massive septic tank two miles distant; recycling; the crematorium; and the raising, slaughtering, and preparation of livestock. A mile away to the north and south, a pair of underground nuclear power plants provided energy for the complex.

Two years after closing the doors to Above Earth, the government decided a more efficient way to run USC7 would be to elect mayors for each section between the intersecting corridors. Each "city" elected two legislators to the lower chamber of the representative council and one to the upper chamber. These chambers coordinated with the Governor. The sections were each given nicknames that meant nothing to Maya—New Boston, New Worcester, New Framingham, New Quincy, New Fall River, New Salem, New Springfield, and New Gloucester.

Crime and disturbances were low, especially after a previous governor had established a red-light district in sub-basement one. Prostitution, alcohol, smoking, and drugs were allowed in this restricted area so long as these guilty pleasures were confined solely to that area and their usage did not detract from a participant's work performance. Most of the facility referred to the district as New Amsterdam, another reference lost on Maya. The penalties for bringing anything from the red-light district back to one's quarters was a loss of privileges for one year and, under extreme cases, banishment from USC7. However, rumors abounded that some of the more discrete working girls and men were occasionally ushered into private quarters on Ring B.

As Maya approached Ring B, an IDF officer blocked her path and raised his hand.

"Sorry, ma'am. Only authorized citizens are allowed in this sector."

"I'm a recruit to the EDF," Maya withdrew her papers and presented them. "I'm trying to get to the ceremony."

The officer glanced at her papers and handed them back. "You better hurry, ma'am. They're about to begin. When you reach Ring A, turn right. It's four doors down on the left. Suite 1105."

"Thanks."

Maya ran down the corridors and entered Suite 1105. A dozen officials and the other recruits milled around the stage. Devon caught her attention and raised his eyebrows in a "where the hell were you" expression. She joined the other recruits as they formed a line in front of the stage. The thirteen officials on the stage–the Governor; her deputy; General Arasaki, the head of the Detachment Forces; Colonels Denning and Roma, the leaders of the EDF and IDF, respectively; and the eight mayors–took their seats as did those in the audience, including her family. General Arasaki rose and approached the podium.

"Please rise for Governor Mangerian."

Everyone stood and applauded. The Governor crossed over to the podium. General Arasaki saluted. She saluted back and shook his hand. As he returned to his seat, the Governor motioned with her hands for the others to sit. When silence filled the auditorium, Mangerian began her speech.

"Ladies and gentlemen, members of the representative councils, and honored guests. We are here today to initiate our eight newest recruits into the Detachment Forces. Let's give them a round of applause."

Everyone in the auditorium stood and turned toward the eight young men and women standing in front of the podium. The applause continued for ten seconds. Maya felt self-conscious.

Mangerian gestured for everyone to be seated and continued.

"Thirty-one years ago next month, we closed the doors to USC7 and abandoned Above Earth. For those of us alive at that time, it had been a heart-wrenching decision to leave behind our usual way of life for an uncertain future. However, a generation later, we are a thriving society, alive and safe. Alive thanks to the determination of everyone who looked to the future with optimism and refused to allow humankind to go extinct. Safe because of the brave men and women who have put their lives in danger to protect our way of life." The Governor turned to the recruits. "You have all chosen to follow an honored tradition by volunteering for the Exterior and Interior Detachment Forces. Colonels Denning and Roma once stood where you are now. A lot will be expected of you. I have complete faith and confidence that you will all perform superbly and will not let us down. Now, please stand and raise your right hands."

The recruits complied.

"Repeat after me. I, state your name, do solemnly swear to protect and defend the citizens of Underground Survival Center 7 against all enemies, interior and exterior, and will do so to the best of my abilities to preserve the remnants of humankind."

Mangerian waited until the recruits responded.

"Congratulations. You're now members of the Detachment

Force."

Another round of applause erupted from the audience. One by one, the thirteen officials left the stage and passed by the cadets, shaking their hands and offering words of encouragement. Arasaki, Denning, and Roma presented each with a crisp salute. When the last of the officials had moved away, the audience moved forward to offer their congratulations.

Maya's mother, Esther, embraced her daughter and hugged her for several seconds. "I'm so proud of you."

"Thanks, Mom." Maya glanced around, grateful to see the other recruits as embarrassed by their parents.

"You did good, kid," said her father, Anthony, who could not get past his wife to hug his daughter. Not that he would have. Her father came from the old school where men loved their families but didn't express their emotions. "I tried to join the IDF once but never made it."

"Really? You never told me that."

"I didn't want to worry you. I knew all along you'd get in. You've always been a tough, smart girl."

"It had nothing to do with being smart," chuckled her younger brother, Carlos. "As the old saying says, it's not who you know but who you blow."

"Are you saying your sister slept her way into this position?" asked a voice from behind Carlos.

Carlos turned around and blanched when he saw Governor Mangerian standing directly behind him. Up close, she appeared far more impressive than the reputation that proceeded her. A small-framed, petite woman now in her sixties, her curly hair cut short and having long ago turned grey, the Governor had been one of the designers of USC7 and knew the facility better than anyone. That knowledge, combined with her determination and zeal for always doing what was right for the citizens of USC7 rather than a particular group, propelled her from one leadership position to another. Eventually, she became governor of USC7 and the only person

14

to have served three terms in that position. Whether the residents like or hated her, everyone respected her.

"Do you think your sister slept her way into this position?" The Governor's gaze bore into Carlos.

"That's not what I meant."

"That's exactly what you meant, and it couldn't be farther from the truth. Devon recommended her, but that didn't guarantee your sister would be recruited." The Governor passed by Carlos without making eye contact, the snub apparent to everyone. She broke into an admiring smile and took Maya's hand. "You earned your position in the EDF. In fact, you placed second on the nomination list sent to the council. You're an ambitious young lady who puts the good of the community over her own needs, and I admire that. I know you're going to be a vital asset. Your family should be proud of you."

"We are," said Anthony.

Esther wrapped a loving arm around Maya's shoulder.

The Governor glanced over at Carlos. "You should *all* be proud of her."

Carlos withered under the stare and fidgeted, his eyes focusing on the floor. "I am."

"You better be." The Governor grinned.

Denning approached the family. "Governor, Mr. and Mrs. Santos. Please excuse me, but the cadets are needed to begin their training."

The Governor squeezed Maya's hand. "Good luck. We're all counting on you."

Esther hugged her daughter. "I'll see you in eight weeks."

"I'll be fine, Mom."

"I know you will." Esther stepped aside and inconspicuously wiped away the tears in her eyes.

This time, Anthony hugged Maya. His voice fought back tears. "I'm so proud of you. I know you'll do great."

"Thanks, Dad."

Carlos embraced her next, though half-heartedly. "I love you."

"I love you, too, runt. Maybe someday you'll get into the EDF."

"And have you boss me around for the rest of my life? No way."

"We have to go," urged Denning.

Maya joined the other cadets. They all chatted excitely amongst themselves as Denning and Roma led them down Ring A. Their euphoria ended when they entered a large gymnasium in the New Quincy sector. The room was massive. The captains closed the door and stood on either side of it, the symbolism overwhelming.

A single person stood in the room. He stood over six feet in height and weighed at least two hundred pounds, all of it muscle. His blonde hair had been shaved into a crew cut. To say he possessed stern features would be an understatement. He glared at them with malicious green eyes.

"God damn. Is this the best you can do?"

"Sorry," replied Denning, suppressing a grin.

"You must have been scraping the lowest levels of the sub-basements for these. They don't even know how to stand at attention."

"Fall in," yelled Roma.

The cadets formed a single line and stood at attention, knowing full well their best would never be good enough. The bear of a man walked down the line slowly, examining each cadet as if they were piles of shit. When he got to the end, he spun around to face them.

"Listen up, you sewer roaches. I'm your drill instructor, Full Sergeant Byrd. For the next nine weeks, I'm your biggest fucking nightmare. I'm going to turn you children into men and women or kill you while trying. You're all full of yourselves because you had a swearing-in ceremony attended by the Governor. I got news for you. That charade was for your families because it'll be the last time some of them will ever see you. You're mine now, and I'm going to whip you into shape. Is that understood?"

"Yes, sir," they said in unison.

"You call that a response? Sewer roaches make more noise than you do. Again."

"Yes, sir." They responded much louder.

Byrd stood in front of Maya, placing his nose inches from hers. "I still can't fucking hear you."

"Yes, sir!" they replied.

"There may be hope for a few of you." Byrd stepped back. He gestured to two tables at the far end of the gymnasium. "Over there are eight sets of uniforms and gym wear, your toiletries, and your ID tags. They are your only possessions for the next eight weeks. Go get them and fall back in."

No one moved.

"Are you waiting for me to say please? Move it!"

The cadets broke rank and ran over to the tables, grabbed their belongings, and headed back to form a line. No one wanted to be last. One cadet, a young boy who shivered in fear, tripped and spilled the clothes and toiletries onto the gym floor.

Byrd ran over to him, shouting, "God fucking damn it."

Maya thought the boy would cry.

"Those items are the property of the USC and are more valuable than you are. What's your name?"

"John Medugno, sir."

The boy collected his stuff.

"Stand at attention when I'm talking to you."

Medugno stood up and snapped rigid. When he did, everything he carried spilled back onto the floor.

"What did you same your name was?"

"John Medugno, sir."

"From now on, it's 'Butterfingers.' Gather your stuff and get into line. Now!"

"Yes, sir." Butterfingers knelt, gathered his belongings, and raced back to the others, berated the entire time.

Once the cadets were in place and at attention, Byrd walked down the ranks. "Behind you are the showers. You're to go in there, store your gear, and change into your gym clothes."

"A unisex shower?" asked the petite blonde girl at the end.

Byrd ran down and stood in front of her, towering over the poor girl.

"Does that bother you, Barbie?"

"No." Her voice quivered.

Byrd's eyes went wide. "No, what?"

"No, sir."

"Then get your asses in there and be back here in five minutes. And God help the last one in line. Move!"

Maya broke into a run and headed for the showers. *What have I gotten myself into?* she thought.

CHAPTER FOUR

M ANGERIAN LEFT THE ceremony and returned to her office. General Arasaki caught up with her halfway down Ring A.

"Thank you for attending the recruitment ceremony, Governor."

She smiled. "It's one of the few ceremonial duties I have to perform I actually enjoy. These people give their lives to keep the rest of us safe."

"I'm afraid we're going to lose a lot more of them before this is through."

Mangerian sighed. "That would be tragic. But I'm more afraid we're going to lose our way of life."

They entered the outer foyer of the Governor's office. Tanner, the receptionist, stood and came around the desk to greet her.

"Everyone is waiting for you."

"Any surprises I should know about?"

"No, ma'am."

"Good."

Mangerian paused by the door to her office, took a few seconds to straighten her clothes and compose herself, then nodded. Tanner opened the door. Mangerian walked in and made her way to the desk against the opposite wall. Across from it sat three cream-colored sofas, one parallel to the Governor's desk and the other two perpendicular and at slight angles. The staff gathered for the meeting rose as Mangerian entered. The Governor greeted them, shaking their hands and exchanging pleasantries, before slipping into her chair. Arasaki sat on the sofa opposite her.

Today's topic of discussion concerned the upcoming elections in six weeks.

"What are the poll numbers?" Mangerian asked.

"Not good," responded Jane Kennedy, her political advisor. A woman in her mid-twenties, Jane was a rising star among political circles. Her intelligence and ability to see an issue from all sides made her invaluable to the government. The citizens liked Jane because of her calm and polite demeanor as well as her youthful look. "Riviera is two points ahead. His campaign is making headway with the voters."

"What parts?" asked Bill Thompson, Mangerian's chief of staff. A heavy-set man with white hair, and only a few years younger than the Governor, he had been a part of the political elite since the first days of USC7. Thompson's former life as a political science professor made him an invaluable asset to the governing bodies.

"All of it. His call for more equitable living standards for the workers is becoming popular."

"Doesn't he realize we're doing all we can?" Thompson spat.

"I can't blame them," said Mangerian. "If I had to spend thirty years living in Ring D, I'd be antsy to move to one of the better rings."

Thompson shook his head. "We've given them everything we can to make their lives better. We've even pretended New Amsterdam doesn't exist."

"It's the housing," countered Jane. "They know how the rest of us live and feel they're entitled to the same standard of living."

"Riviera's inciting a class war."

Mangerian ignored her chief of staff. "Is there any way we could move the families into better accommodations?"

"We could," Jane offered. "There are some empty quarters

in Ring C, but not enough to house all the families. To do that, we'd have to ask single people in Ring C to double up. That would open enough spaces for the working families."

"That would piss off those who support you," suggested Thompson.

"And it wouldn't do much to relieve the situation of single workers," Jane continued. "Even if we spread out the single workers into the family spaces, we'd still be looking at three or four to a room."

Mangerian thought for a moment. "What if we lessened the size of each room in Ring D and gave everyone their own space?"

"The rooms would be small. We would need to build more communal areas for them."

The Governor focused her attention on Jeff Donahue, the Administrator of the Interior.

"We have the resources and the space," he said. "It would take eighteen months to complete."

"This is a problem we should hand over to the mayors," suggested Thompson. "Let them work out the details. They'll take all the crap from those citizens unhappy about the situation while you'll get the credit for initiating the change."

"He has a point," added Jane.

Mangerian paused. "Then we'll announce it a week after the elections."

"Maybe we should announce it now."

Thompson shook his head. "It'll only look like a half-assed solution to a perceived problem. That will cost us votes. We should wait until after the elections to announce it."

"Agreed," said the Governor. "What else?"

"Riviera is also pushing to spend fewer resources on the defense forces. He doesn't feel they're necessary anymore."

"He's an ass," replied Thompson.

Mangerian agreed with both Riviera and Thompson on this issue. Crime had never been over one percent in USC7.

Most of the calls handled by the Internal Defense Force pertained to domestic disputes and the occasional fist fight, all of which had been on the rise in the last few years. Not that she could blame them considering the conditions everyone lived under. She seriously doubted decreasing the number of IDF personnel would negatively impact the compound. Besides, those IDF officers inside USC7 were needed outside.

"Agreed. Tell the IDF half of them will be transferred to the EDF. Ask for volunteers first. We can assign personnel if not enough willingly agree to transfer over. Keep the transfer secret. Announce on Thursday that we'll be cutting back on the size of the IDF. Also, make it clear that we'll reinstate those numbers to their original level if crime increases. We don't want the citizens to worry."

"Gotcha."

"Any other good news?"

Jane swallowed hard. "Riviera's open-door policy is also gaining traction."

Arasaki shook his head. "That won't work."

"Maybe not," continued Jane. "But after the incident four weeks ago, his proposal is becoming popular with the voters."

Arasaki seemed dumbfounded. "He's talking about that?"

Jane nodded.

"The son of a bitch should be arrested for revealing classified information."

"Normally, I'd agree with you," said Thompson. "But any action like that now would be perceived as a political move against Riviera. The more people who find out about it, the more this administration seems cruel."

"Cruel?" blurted Arasaki. "We can't allow in outsiders, especially now. It could disrupt what we have."

Jane interrupted the argument. "They don't see it that way. They view it as a harsh move on our part. The Governor dropped five points in the polls because of it."

Mangerian sighed. The incident referred to took place a

month ago when a family of five arrived at the entrance to USC7 seeking shelter. They claimed to have been surviving on their own for years. Plausible but, under the current circumstances, suspicious. She had denied Denning's request to allow them into the facility. He gave them a week's worth of food and water and sent them on their way. She hated having to do it because her actions were callous. The family had probably died by now. However, if they were marauders, allowing them in could have compromised the integrity of the facility. What could she do? As that old TV show used to say, logic dictates the needs of the many outweigh the needs of the few.

"How are we handling the publicity on that?"

All eyes turned to Arasaki.

"I issued a statement confirming the incident and stating we had to turn them away because our resources were already strained."

"Which made us look like assholes," responded Thompson.

Jane nodded in agreement.

Mangerian leaned back in her chair and closed her eyes. Part of her wished she would lose this election so she could put all this shit behind her. Yet, she had a responsibility to keep the citizens of USC7 safe. She opened her eyes and faced her staff.

"There's nothing we can do about it now. After the election, I'll form a team to investigate the matter. We'll blame it on miscommunication and too strong an adherence to the rules. I'll make a promise to do better in the future and judge future incidents on a case-by-case basis."

"That's the best approach," said Thompson. "Assuming we win in six weeks."

"We have to win." Mangerian didn't need to add that the future of USC7 depended on it.

CHAPTER FIVE

TODAY HAD BEEN hell. Byrd started their ordeal by making them run laps around the gymnasium until none of them could stand. As each one dropped out of line, the drill instructor berated them for being lazy sewer roaches and telling them they did not belong in his defense forces. Of course, Butterfinger dropped out first, earning a seething tirade that only intensified as the others called it quits.

Then the cadets performed an endless series of push-ups, sit-ups, and jumping jacks that drained them of energy. Still, they refused to give up. No one wanted to provide Byrd with an excuse to bully them even more. Everyone wanted to prove to themself that they could handle whatever the drill instructor threw at them.

After two hours of being physically tested beyond their limits, Byrd took them to the chow hall for dinner, back to the gym to gather their gear, and introduced them to their barracks.

Eight cots sat on the floor, four on either side of the aisle, with a wall locker to the right of each cot and a footlocker at the end. The furnishings seemed as old as the facility itself. Most of the others groaned on seeing it. Not Maya. These were standard living conditions in Ring D. In fact, she had more personal space here than she did at her parents' place.

"Pick a bunk and fall in," Byrd bellowed.

Everyone grabbed a cot, placed their gear on the mattress, and stood at attention. Medugno's pile of clothes fell onto their side.

Byrd was on him faster than a fly on shit. "Is that how you treat government property, Butterfingers?"

"No, sir." Medugno stood there, staring at the drill instructor.

"Fix it!"

Medugno spun around, restacked the clothes properly, and stood back at attention.

Byrd shook his head and strolled back and forth along the aisle. "All right, people. This is your home for the next eight weeks. I don't know how your mommies let you live, but here everything will be spotless and in order. If I find anything out of place, your parents will never see you again. Is that clear?"

"Yes, sir."

"I can't hear you!"

"Sir, yes, sir."

"You have thirty minutes to shower and stow your gear before lights out. Dismissed."

Byrd strutted out of the barracks and entered the room across the corridor.

"We ought to get to know each other since we'll be going through the same hell for the next eight weeks." The comment came from the tallest member of the cadets, who stood at six feet two inches, black, handsome, and possessing piercing brown eyes. "I'm Richard Carver from Ring C. My family runs a clothing store in New Salem."

"Why did you join?" asked Maya.

"I wanted to do my part. My folks were against me signing up. They want me to take over the family business. To be honest, doing that would bore me to death. Someday I hope to see Above Earth."

A murmur of understanding came from the other cadets.

Barbie spoke next. She stood five and a half feet tall, a petite woman with long blonde hair and perfect skin. "I'm Jaime Simmons from Ring B in New Gloucester. My father made me join."

"Is he former defense forces?" asked Carver.

"No." Jaime shook her head. "He's one of the elected officials in New Gloucester. He thought it would look bad if the elites didn't participate in the dirty work. His words, not mine. I'm an only child, so I had the honor."

"I'm Rudolph Sanchez." Sanchez had a toughness about him, both in his appearance and demeanor. Just under six feet in height, with olive skin and blue eyes, he looked and sounded tough, like he had been raised in a tough neighborhood. "My family was originally from Puerto Rico before we moved to Cambridge. My old man is an electrician. I followed in his footsteps. We ran our own business and were lucky enough to be selected. I don't plan on staying in Ring C for the rest of my life. This is my only way to better my status, so none of you assholes better fuck it up." Sanchez cast Butterfingers a hateful glare.

"Leave him alone," said the brunette. "It's only his first day."

"Who's going to make me," Sanchez said defiantly.

Carver positioned himself between the two and stared down Sanchez. "I am."

Sanchez waved off Carver and went back to stowing his gear.

Carver turned to the brunette and smiled. "I'll give you this. You got balls."

"My father wished I had. He always wanted a son and instead got a daughter. I'm Bettany Daniels." Bettany was attractive but not in the way Jaime carried it. Tall, just under six feet, with long brunette hair and stunning green eyes, she had long limbs and an elongated face. "My parents are teachers in New Framingham. I'm supposed to be a teacher myself, but my grades are underwater. Below C level. My choices were either join the defense forces or be consigned to Ring E."

Butterfingers went next. "I'm John Medugno from Ring C.

26

My father died when I was young. I never knew him. My mother works for the mayor of New Fall River. I have no skills—"

"No fucking shit," mumbled Sanchez.

"—so, I joined the defense forces. I'm beginning to think I made a mistake."

"Don't sweat it, man," said Carver. "You'll get the hang of it."

"I hope so."

"And you?" Carver asked the chubby cadet.

The cadet stood at five feet seven inches with a slight paunch. He had a round face, brown eyes, and dark blonde hair cut short. Although not as attractive as Carver or Sanchez, no one would define him as ugly. His sullen and depressed appearance detracted from his demeanor, as if he did not want to be here.

"I'm Henry Bodman. My old man retired from the IDF several years ago. He sees me as a disappointment. Calls me fat, dumb, and lazy."

"I wonder why?" Sanchez chuckled.

"That's enough out of you." Carver flashed Sanchez a glare that quieted the asshole.

"I may be fat, but I'm far from lazy. Or dumb. I had a 3.96 average in high school."

Carver nodded. "So, you're here to prove him wrong?"

"Screw my old man. I'm here to prove to myself I can hack it."

"I'm Nori." The young Asian man gave the group a half-hearted wave.

"Do you have a last name?" asked Bettany.

Nori hesitated before replying, "Arasaki."

Jaime raised her head and focused on Nori. "General Arasaki is your father?"

"Grandfather, to be exact. My family has been in the military since World War II. My great-grandfather served with the

442nd Infantry Regiment that fought in Italy. All the men in the family have served since then. But please, don't hold it against me."

"Why would we hold it against you?" asked Bodman.

"Because traditionally drill instructors are tougher on cadets who come from military lineage to prove they're not showing favoritism."

"Fucking great," mumbled Sanchez.

Everyone ignored him.

"I promise I won't let you down," said Nori.

"I'm sure you won't." Carver moved over to Maya. "So that means you're our recruit from Ring D. Congratulations."

"Why are you congratulating her?" asked Jaime.

"Because she's the first recruit ever to join the defense forces from the lower ranks." Carver made quotation marks with his fingers on the last two words to show he did not mean the term disrespectfully.

"That's me. I'm Maya Santos. My family has been living in Ring D since the Great Freeze. I'm lucky to be here."

"We're lucky to have you," said Carver.

As they went back to stowing their gear, Sanchez made his way over and invaded Maya's personal space.

"Don't worry," he whispered. "We'll show these white folks what we're made of."

If she had not done so already, she would have taken an instant dislike for Sanchez. He was an asshole and a racist. She had once heard her father say all assholes in the military are fragged to prevent them from getting the unit killed. She had no idea what her father meant by that. But if anyone deserved to be fragged, it would be Sanchez.

CHAPTER SIX

MAYA AND THE other cadets rose at 0600 when reveille blasted over the loudspeakers of their barracks. The lights came on, revealing Byrd standing at one end of the aisle holding a heavily dented metal trash can and a stick. Byrd walked down the cots, banging the stick inside the trash can.

"What is wrong with you people? Even sewer roaches react when the lights go on. Move it!"

Maya jumped up and stood at attention. Out of the corner of her eye, she watched Byrd reach the opposite end of the aisle, drop the trash can onto the floor, and toss the stick inside with a loud clang. Glancing to her right, she noticed Medugno sound asleep in his cot. She went to wake him but stopped when Byrd spun around and yelled, "Attention!"

Byrd walked back down the aisle.

"Sound off."

Each cadet yelled out their name as the drill instructor passed. No one answered when he arrived at Medugno's cot. Byrd stared at him, astounded that the cadet had slept through the wake-up. He picked up the end of the cot, raised it six inches, and dropped it.

Medugno rolled onto his back and snored.

Byrd raised and dropped the cot a second time.

Medugno opened his eyes. "Morning, Sarge."

"Morning, Butterfingers." Byrd smiled and sounded almost friendly. "Did you sleep well?"

"I did, thanks."

"Good." The smile faded from Byrd's face. "You missed

roll call, you pathetic excuse of a cadet. Out of bed and in line. Now!"

Medugno jumped off his cot and stumbled, the blanket still wrapped around him. He snapped to attention in front of the drill instructor, the blanket draped around his feet.

"Are you bringing your blankie with you?"

"No, sir."

"Then put it in bed where it belongs!"

Medugno crouched, picked up the blanket, tossed it on the cot, and stood back at attention in one fluid motion.

Several of the cadets snickered, including Maya. Byrd moved in front of her, his face inches from hers.

"You think this is fucking funny?"

"No, sir."

"Then why did you laugh?"

"I don't know."

"What?"

"I don't know, sir."

Byrd spun around and made his way across to Barbie. "Do you think I'm a fucking clown here to amuse you?"

"No, sir."

Byrd stepped away and proceeded down the aisle. "Maybe it's time we work some of that humor out of you sewer roaches. Meet me in the gym in five minutes. Full fatigues."

"What about breakfast?" asked Bodman.

"How careless of me to forget." Byrd's voice dripped with sarcasm. "Porky is right. Breakfast is the most important meal of the day. Get your sorry asses to the chow hall and meet me in forty-five minutes in the gym in full fatigues."

Maya had a bad feeling.

✧   ✧   ✧

MAYA'S PREDICTION CAME to pass. When the cadets arrived at the gym, Byrd waited for them with eight backpacks, each filled with one hundred pounds of weight. He made each cadet put on one then run ten laps around the gym at double time. The punishment was bad enough. Right after eating, it became excruciating. Fortunately, she had only a slice of toast and some orange juice. Those who ate a full meal paid heavily for the luxury.

Bettany dropped out on the second lap, vomiting on the floor. Byrd rushed over, berated her for being weak, gave her the nickname "Pukes," and sent her back with three additional laps added to her punishment.

Sanchez heaved up his breakfast on lap five. Byrd ran up to him before he finished emptying his stomach. "What the hell are you doing? That's a waste of food."

Sanchez wiped his mouth and struggled to his feet. "Sorry, sir."

"I'm sure the farmers in the sub-basement will forgive you. But I won't. Get back in and give me four extra laps."

By lap eight, Maya felt as if she would collapse at any moment. Every muscle ached. She hated to think what they would feel like in the morning. Every cadet panted and breathed heavily. Even Carver, the tallest and strongest of the group, began to blanch. The unit had degraded from a firm line running double-time to a scattered mass barely plodding along.

Byrd appeared beside them.

"You people are a disgrace. Back in line and double-time unless you want to do this again."

Two more laps of torment were preferable to repeating this nightmare, so they fell into formation and picked up the pace. Carver threw up while he ran, covering the front of his fatigues in vomit.

The drill instructor descended on him like a bird of prey. "Is that how you show respect for the USC uniform by puking on it?"

"No, sir." Carver gagged.

"Someone is going to have to wash that. You think they

want to clean up your puke?"

"No, sir." With his stomach empty, Carver picked up the pace. "It won't happen again."

"You're damn right it won't. Give me five extra laps. Move!"

At the end of the tenth lap, Maya slowed and slid off the backpack. She swore her shoulder and back muscles sighed with relief. Two others had completed the laps before her and already sat on the floor, gasping for breath, their faces and fatigues soaked with sweat. When the last four joined them, Byrd came over.

"Okay, people. You can rest over there." He pointed to eight metal folding chairs set up in the center of the gym in front of a large screen TV on a movable cart. "Colonel Denning and Colonel Roma want to talk to you."

The five cadets made their way to the chairs and sat down. For a moment, Maya forgot about what she had been through, relieved to be off her feet for a few minutes. Bettany and Sanchez joined them fifteen minutes later. Carver shortly after that. He sat beside Maya. She could smell the vomit on his fatigues.

Byrd stepped up in front of them. "So that you know, the ten laps were because of Butterfingers. Doing it on a full stomach was because of Porky." He glared at the two men. "Maybe next time you two sewer roaches will think before you fuck it up for everyone."

"Yes, sir," replied Bodman.

Medugno lowered his head.

"Listen up while they brief you. After that, your asses are mine." Byrd turned to the officers and saluted. "They're all yours, sirs."

Roma stood in front of the cadets. "I need a half-hour of your time. And pay attention because this is important. We're going to show you a program explaining why the EDF and IDF are so important. Listen carefully. If you have any questions,

Colonel Denning and I will answer them after the presentation."

Denning walked over to the TV, ejected the DVD holder, slid a disk into the empty slot, and closed it.

"This presentation is classified and cannot be discussed outside the defense forces or the government."

The screen flickered for a few moments and then brightened. A blue background appeared on the screen, followed by the words:

A HISTORY OF
USC7 AND
THE EDF/IDF

CHAPTER SEVEN

THE IMAGE OF a middle-aged man with grey hair appeared on the screen. He wore a dark suit, white shirt, and red tie. He appeared well-groomed and his demeanor professional, although dark circles under his eyes and age lines across his forehead indicated he had been through a lot. Maya recognized his face from her history classes in school.

Welcome to your training to become members of the External and Internal Defense Forces. I'm Richard Flynn, the first governor of USC7. You are here because you were the most qualified among those who applied. Congratulations on being accepted. And thank you. Your service ensures that the citizens of USC7 will remain safe and enjoy the democracy and prosperity left over from Above Earth. However, you will also play a much more vital role in defending USC7 that only those in the defense forces and top government officials know about.

The image switched from Governor Flynn to a montage of beautiful scenic views, vibrant images of city life, and people enjoying life outdoors.

We all miss Above Earth. The weather. The seasons. The ability to walk around outside and travel. And we'll miss it for the rest of our lives. The sad truth is that while we enjoyed the life provided by Above Earth, we took advantage of it.

The pleasant images switched to disturbing ones of densely populated urban areas, forest harvesting, barren agricultural fields, empty store shelves, large-scale migrant movement, and melting ice caps.

In the decade before the Great Freeze, governments around the world turned a blind eye to the havoc humans were causing on our planet.

Overpopulation placed increasing strains on resources, especially food, fresh water, and energy. The deforesting of the Amazon rain forest and other areas disrupted the ecosystem. Mass migrations merely moved the economic burden from nations unable to handle the strain to others that eventually weakened under the pressure. All this was accelerated by, and in many cases contributed to, changes in our climate. By the time the world took notice and began to act, many believed it was already too late.

The video showed exterior shots of two scientific institutions and scenes of Asians and Americans working.

Scientists around the world studied ways to reverse the more adverse effects of climate change. A research team from the United States, Russia, and Japan developed the idea of generating phytoplankton, or algae, by infusing the oceans to increase its growth in the hopes that the algae would absorb the excess CO_2 from the atmosphere. Meanwhile, a second team composed of scientists from China and India figured out a way to stop the melting of the polar ice caps by pumping seawater into the air, allowing the salt crystals to seed with the low-altitude clouds and reflect sunlight. The intent was to cool off the planet by several degrees to restore the polar ice caps and create more arable land to increase food production. Both sets of intentions were noble. However, no one could have predicted the outcome.

Images appeared of the Great Freeze. Cities and country sides covered in yards of snow. Highways snowed under, with the traffic covered in mounds of white. Entire towns buried. Endless images of the dead, killed by the cold.

Denning and Roma twinged.

Temperatures did decline by several degrees. For a while, the situation improved. However, once the process started, it could not be reversed. CO_2 levels dropped from four hundred and fifteen parts per million down to two hundred and fifty, then down to one hundred and seventy parts per million. World temperatures continued to decline. Snow became common, even in temperate climates. Blizzards wracked the northern and southern hemispheres, making it impossible to grow food or raise livestock. Processed foods could not keep up with the demand. Hunger prevailed, even in First World countries. The Third World suffered devastating losses to their *populations. The United Nations declared a global state of emergency. It's estimated that world temperatures will fall as low as negative fifty degrees Fahrenheit. Once it became apparent life could no longer be sustained above ground, the world decided to act.*

An awkward edit occurred in the presentation, followed by scenes of the construction of USC7.

We built USC7 in the design of the Pentagon, only much larger to accommodate two million people. We provided everything necessary to sustain a society underground—housing, food, supplies, nuclear energy, and, most importantly, our democracy. I'd be lying if I said life won't be difficult for those who survive. But we will survive, and we will prosper.

The presentation shifted back to Governor Flynn.

That's where you, the men and women of the Defense Forces, will play a vital role. You'll be responsible for ensuring domestic tranquility within USC7 and protecting the facility from external threats, if there are any. As cliché as it sounds, you are the first line of defense. You may have to perform unpleasant tasks, and many may consider you the enemy, but I know you'll all do your duty.

May God bless USC7. And may God bless the men and women of the Defense Forces.

The presentation ended. Denning walked over and shut off the television.

"Are there any questions?"

There were many.

Medugno raised his hand. "What did he mean by we may have to perform unpleasant tasks and we may be considered by many to be an enemy?"

"The governor made that video during the first week here. At the time, we expected civil unrest among the citizens. Thankfully, that never happened."

"And external threats?" asked Barbie.

"Back then, there were many people not selected for USC7 that resented being excluded. We experienced over a dozen raids by outsiders trying to take over the facility in those first months. One raid consisted of three thousand people. I was a cadet in the EDF at the time. I never want to live through that again."

Barbie asked a follow-up question. "What happened to the outsiders?"

"They had to fend for themselves."

"You mean they were left them outside to freeze?" Bodman asked in an accusatory tone.

"Yes." Denning lowered his head.

"That's what the governor meant by unpleasant tasks," Roma interjected from behind them. He walked around to face the cadets. "You must remember, the engineers precisely calculated everything to accommodate two million citizens. Adding an extra three thousand or more people could have upset the balance and led to failure. No one at the time in the... no one in USC7 could be certain we would survive a few months. The fact we've lasted thirty-one years is a miracle."

"Thanks to people like you," added Denning.

"Why do we still need an EDF?" asked Bettany. "Do we still face external threats?"

"Mostly from polar bears."

"Polar bears?" Nori sounded incredulous. "This far south?"

Denning nodded. "They're used to the weather. Their numbers multiplied once man was removed from the ecosystem. When their food supplies in the Arctic were gone, they wandered south in search of food."

"Has the EDF run into any?" Carver inquired.

"Yes," answered Roma.

"In fact," added Denning, "over the years, we've lost almost a dozen people on perimeter patrol to polar bear attacks. So long as we see them first, we're fine. But they've learned to camouflage themselves under the snow and strike without warning."

"Shit," mumbled Medugno.

"You said mostly polar bears, which implies other external threats." The statement came from Sanchez.

Denning sighed. "We've had marauders… people from Above Earth who somehow survived the cold… who have tried to break in and have had to be repelled."

Barbie bristled. "Like that family of five that we turned away last month?"

Denning avoided her gaze.

"That was a mistake," Roma said forcefully. "The moment the Governor found out they had been turned away, she sent the EDF to look for them. We never found them."

Maya sensed the colonel was lying.

Denning spoke up. "In the future, anyone seeking asylum will be vetted and granted access on a case-by-case basis. But we still need to refuse entry to anyone who tries to break in. Any more questions?"

"I have one," said Maya. "How were the citizens of USC7 selected amongst those still alive?"

"Very carefully," joked Roma, who changed his tone when the humor fell flat. "We denied a pass to anyone with a record of criminal violence. The rest were chosen based on whether their skills would be an asset to the community. Farmers, livestock breeders, engineers, medical personnel, teachers, people like that. As you know, everyone in USC7 contributes for the greater good."

"Some more than others," said Sanchez.

Roma bristled. "What does that mean?"

"The politicians don't do any of the manual labor. They sit around all day and tell us what to do."

Denning interrupted before the situation devolved into a shouting match. "The politicians maintain order and try to accommodate the will of the people. We've maintained our way of life because of them."

"You don't want Ring D running the show, do you?" Roma glanced over at Maya, recognizing he had spoken without thinking. He averted his gaze.

"Yes," added Denning. "There are a few on the council

who are of little use, mostly billionaires who helped pay to build USC7 and were granted a pass."

"You mean they bought their way to safety?" asked Maya.

"They financed the operation so millions of others might live." Denning's tone signified the discussion had come to an end.

Roma took over. "Grab lunch and be at the shooting range at 1300 sharp for weapon training. Dismissed."

The cadets snapped to attention, saluted, and waited for the captains to leave before heading for the chow. Maya hoped her impertinence would not come back to haunt her.

CHAPTER EIGHT

THE RUSTLING OF cots woke Maya from her sleep. She wrote it off as her fellow cadets stirring, but then she heard whispering. Two figures stood at the end of her cot. She opened her eyes. Medugno and Bodman were conspiring.

"It's too risky," said Bodman.

"Are you hungry? Don't you want a snack?"

"Yes, but what if we get caught?"

"Byrd is sound asleep," said Medugno. "He won't know it happened."

"What are you two up to?" asked Maya. She startled the two cadets.

"Why are you awake?" asked Medugno.

"Because you two idiots woke me. What's going on?"

"We're hungry," Bodman answered. "There are snacks in the drill instructor's break room. We're going to sneak a few."

"Are you insane? You'll get caught."

"No, we won't. Byrd's asleep."

"Unless you rat us out," added Medugno.

"Leave me out of this." Maya rolled over in her bunk and faced the other way. "You're on your own."

Medugno and Bodman snuck over to the door. Maya waited until they left before lying on her back so she could watch this idiocy play out.

Bodman cracked open the barracks door and peered out. Byrd's door was closed tight. Bodman opened his wider and peered out. Medugno slinked out and made his way to the drill instructor's lounge only fifty feet away. A minute later, Bodman anxiously waved for him to hurry.

As Medugno raced into the barracks, the door to Byrd's quarters swung open. He wore sweatpants and a t-shirt.

"I thought I smelled the stench of sewer roaches in my fine corridor. What the Hell are you two doing?"

Medugno tossed his stash onto the floor beside him. "We were just getting some air, sir."

"Bullshit. I was born at night, just not last night." Byrd stepped into the barracks and switched on the lights. His eyes immediately fell on the snacks scattered across the tiles. "Is that how you treat government property?"

"No, sir."

"What are you waiting for? Pick it up."

As Medugno dropped to his hands and knees gathering the snacks, Byrd turned on Bodman. "Go get the rest of them."

"What?"

"Am I speaking in a foreign language, Porky, or are your ears so filled with lard you can't hear me? Go get the rest of the snacks."

By now, the rest of the cadets were out of bed and had fallen in at attention at the end of their bunks. Each knew this would not end well.

Bodman rushed in from the drill instructors lounge, the snacks piled in the pouch he made from his t-shirt. Medugno stood up, stumbling. Thankfully for him, he did not drop any.

Byrd stared at the two thieves. "Well, fall in with the others."

When Medugno and Bodman reached their bunks, the two cadets realized they could not stand at attention holding their stash, so they dropped the snacks on their bunks and came to attention.

Byrd paced the aisle. "Apparently, the fine cooks of the defense forces are slacking in their efforts because Butterfingers and Porky are still hungry. Do you all agree?"

"Sir, no, sir."

Byrd stopped in front of Bettany. "Did you know about this?"

"No, sir."

He spun around and got into Maya's face. "Did you?"

Maya could not tell if he knew or was testing her. In either case, honesty was the best policy. "Yes, sir. I did."

"And you did nothing to stop it?"

"I advised them against it."

Byrd got into her face. "And why didn't you tell me?"

"Because snitches get stitches, sir."

The slightest hint of a smile pierced his lips. "At least you show some integrity. There may be hope for you bunch of losers yet."

Moving down to the end of the aisle, Byrd spun around. "Go ahead, cadets. Dig in."

Carver glanced over at the drill instructor. "Excuse me, sir?"

"Did I suddenly go mute? I said, dig in. Butterfingers and Porky brought snacks. It's only right that they share them."

The cadets hesitated.

"Eat! And make sure nothing is wasted."

The cadets ran toward the two bunks and picked a snack. Medugno and Bodman dug into the pile and wolved down food as if they hadn't eaten in days. Jaime joined in. Maya, Bettany, Sanchez, and Carver grabbed a protein bar and chewed slowly, not wanting to fill up. Realizing what would happen next, Nori slowed down, taking ten minutes to eat an apple.

When the cadets consumed the last snack, most of it by Medugno and Bodman, Byrd walked down the aisle.

"Was that good, cadets?"

"Yes, sir."

Byrd smiled. He shook his body and rubbed his stomach as he strolled by the bunks. "Bellies nice and full?"

"Yes, sir."

"Good." The drill instructor stopped and turned to face them. "Now it's time we work off those extra carbs. We're going to do a lap around Ring E. Don't want to wake the fine citizens of this facility by having you pigs stampeding through the halls. Anytime someone pukes, I'll add a lap to everyone. Now move!"

The cadets filed out of the barracks in their skivvies and bare feet, with Byrd behind them. When they reached Ring E, Byrd yelled, "Repeat after me. I'm a pig, but I don't care."

"I'm a pig, but I don't care."

"Everybody got their share."

"Everybody got their share."

It took almost two hours to complete the lap. They passed by nightshift workers who applauded and jeered, the humiliation adding to their misery. No one puked. Medugno almost did but swallowed the barf rising in his throat before the drill instructor noticed.

By the time they returned to the barracks, sweaty and exhausted, they had less than three hours until reveille.

CHAPTER NINE

LIKE ALL CADETS, today's training excited Maya. Citizens of USC7 were prohibited from owning any type of firearms. Only defense force personnel had access to them, which made them like forbidden fruit. She stared at the three weapons laid out on the table in front of her–a knife, a sidearm, and the primary weapon. She could hardly wait to get her hands on them.

Byrd entered the gym and made his way to the opposite side of the table. The cadets snapped to attention.

"At ease."

The cadets stood with their legs apart and their hands folded behind their back.

"All right, sewer roaches. Today you take a step up on the food chain. We're going to learn about the weapons you'll be carrying while on duty and the rules you must adhere to when carrying them."

Byrd grabbed the primary weapon and held it out in front of him in his right hand, the muzzle pointed to his right. As he spoke, he used his left to point out the features he discussed.

"This is an M4 Carbine. It's a gas-operated automatic weapon. The M4 uses 5.56x45 mm rounds, has a firing rate of nine hundred fifty rounds per minute, a muzzle velocity of one thousand nine hundred feet per second, and a range of six hundred yards. It is your best friend. You will each be issued one for the duration of your training. Though there are many like it, the one you'll be issued is yours. You will treat that weapon better than you do your parents or loved ones because they won't save your life when the shit hits the fan. This will."

Byrd placed down the M4 and picked up the sidearm.

"This is your secondary weapon. It's a Sig Sauer M17 semi-automatic pistol. It's a recoil-operated weapon. The M17 uses 9x19 mm Parabellum rounds, V-Crown, 124 grain. It has a muzzle velocity of twelve hundred feet per second and a range of fifty yards. You will use it if your primary weapon fails or you run out of ammunition. It's also highly effective for close-quarters combat. The magazine holds twenty hollow point rounds and shoots at a rate of nine hundred rounds a minute. To put it in terms you'll understand, a hollow point bullet makes a small hole when it enters the body and a large hole when it exits. It's quite useful for when your enemy gets close."

"Enemies, sir?" asked Sanchez.

"Polar bears. They're near the top of the food chain. Un-trained cadets are like a burrito to them. Hot and tasty."

Byrd turned his attention back to the table, placing down the M17 and picking up the knife.

"This is a Ka-Bar combat and utility knife. Hopefully, you'll never have to use this in combat because it means you are close and personal with the enemy, and polar bears have a huge advantage over us. We'll train on this later. For now, all you need to know is that the best way to use the knife is to plunge it into your target to the hilt." Byrd displayed its use. "Turn the blade one hundred and eighty degrees. Then pull it up and out so the serrated edge does the most damage."

"What if it doesn't bring down a polar bear?" asked Barbie.

"Then your best bet is to spread your legs, put your head between them, and kiss your ass goodbye."

Maya suppressed a snicker.

Byrd replaced the knife with the M4. "There are four rules you must follow when using the M4 and the M17. When handling a firearm, you will remove the magazine." Again, the drill instructor went through the motions as he lectured. "Rule two, you will pull back the slide and check the barrel to ensure there is no round in the chamber. You will look away and check it a second time. Rule three, once you insert the magazine and load a round into the chamber, you will lock the safety to ensure no accidental discharge. Is that clear?"

"Yes, sir."

Byrd tossed the M4 to Medugno. "Butterfingers, show me how it's done."

Medugno looked to his right and left at the cadets beside him, then turned at a ninety-degree angle. With the muzzle pointed at the floor, he removed the magazine and slipped it into his pocket. Pulling back the slide, he checked the chamber. A round sat inside the weapon. Medugno removed it, turned his head away, then rechecked the chamber. Reinserting the magazine, he loaded a round in the chamber, flipped on the safety, then faced forward holding the weapons in both hands, the muzzle pointed toward the ceiling.

"I'm impressed," said Byrd with a nod of satisfaction. "There may be hope for you yet. Put the weapon back on the table."

Medugno obeyed, setting down the Carbine so the barrel faced away from Byrd at an angle.

"Very good, Butterfingers. Now, what's rule number four?"

A pause hung over the cadets. Finally, Barbie asked, "Keep your weapon clean?"

"That's a good guess, but it's a given. Does anyone else have brain cells that are working?"

"Never point your weapon at anyone?" Bettany said hesitantly.

"Are you asking me or telling me?"

"Never point your weapon at anyone, sir."

"Very good. You win a cookie. Cadet Daniels is correct. The barrel of your weapons should never point at anything you don't intend to shoot or kill. The defense forces have lost more people to misuse of their weapons than to polar bear attacks. Remember these four rules. Each of you is allowed one screw-up. On the second offense, you wash out. Is that clear?"

"Yes, sir," the cadets replied.

"I can't hear you."

"Sir, yes, sir!"

"Good. These are the weapons you'll eventually be assigned. Follow me."

Byrd led the way to the opposite side of the gym. Another table sat on the floor covered by a large cloth. Beyond it stood eight dummies shaped like humans. Denning and Roma stood on either end of the table. When the cadets formed a line, the two captains moved behind them.

Byrd stepped up to the other end of the table. "These are what you'll be training on."

He removed the cloth, revealing eight paintball guns laying on the surface. A collective moan rose from the ranks. Maya had not been this disappointed since she had failed that pop quiz in history class.

"Don't get whiny on me. Ammunition is at a premium. We're not going to waste it on you sewer roaches until you can at least hit your target. There are fifty rounds in each weapon. You will be ranked by the number that hit a vital spot on the dummies, the number that hit the target, and the number of misses. For your sake, the latter number better be low." Byrd joined the two captains behind the cadets. "Begin."

The cadets each picked up a paintball gun and began firing. Most did poorly at first, missing the targets. The wooden background had so much paint splattered on it that it looked like a piece of artwork, and a bad one at that. Maya noticed each cadet had different colored bullets, making their misses stand out.

"People, you're not firing into a zombie horde. You have a single target, so aim carefully."

By the last thirty rounds, they began hitting their marks. Paint coated the dummies. When finished, they placed down their weapons and stood at ease for the others to finish.

Medugno finished last. They waited for the results to be tallied.

Byrd took up his position behind the table, this time holding a clipboard.

"Sanchez, you scored 19/21/10. Not bad, but you can do better."

"Thank you, sir."

"Barbie, you scored 5/18/27. Congratulations, you're the worst shot in the class."

For a moment, Maya thought Barbie would break into tears.

Byrd made his way down the line reading the scores. Bodman: 12/29/9. Arasaki: 23/20/7. Medugno: 22/19/9. Carver: 25/17/8. Bettany: 29/15/6.

Byrd stopped in front of Maya and fixated on her.

"How did I do, sir?"

"You scored 46/4/0. Damn impressive."

"And six of those were headshots," added Denning.

"You're a natural at this," said Byrd.

"I practiced a lot as a kid. I used to kill sewer rats with a BB gun."

Maya immediately regretted her last comment. BB guns were among the prohibited weapons in USC7. The gym went quiet as everyone waited for the tirade.

Denning spoke first. "You do realize BB guns are illegal?"

"Yes, sir."

"Step over here." Roma walked until halfway across the gym. Maya followed with Denning a few steps behind her.

"Heads up, people," ordered Byrd. "You've never seen anyone get their ass chewed before? Round two of target practice. And this time, try to hit something other than the backdrop."

Maya reached Roma and waited for the dressing down. The colonel did not disappoint her.

"You realize using a prohibited weapon inside is not only grounds for drumming you out of the defense forces but could also get you and your family banned from the facility."

"My family had nothing to do with this, sir, so please don't punish them?"

"Where did you get the BB gun?" asked Denning.

"I found it," Maya lied. Her father had smuggled it in to kill any rats that might make their way into the apartment. He had hidden it away and never used it but was too afraid to turn it in to the authorities. She had discovered it by accident and had been using it since she turned thirteen.

"Where did you find it?" asked Roma.

"Down in the sub-basement. I used to go down there a lot after school to see what went on. I found it beside a locker and started using it to kill sewer rats. I figured there'd be no harm in that." At least she didn't lie about the latter part.

"What do you suggest we do?" Roma asked Denning.

The colonel looked Maya up and down, making a show of it. Finally, he responded. "Well, she did use it only to kill vermin that we exterminate anyway. She was too young to know better. Besides, it made her a crack shot. If I ran into a polar bear, I'd rather have her beside me than the others."

Maya caught Roma winking at Denning. "She's your cadet, so I'll stay out of it. I would hate to see her drummed out over something so minor."

"Thank you, sir."

"I'm the one you should be thanking," snapped Denning.

"Sorry, sir. Thank you, sir."

"That's better." Denning repressed a grin. "Now join the others and show them how it's done. And I want to see that forty-two up to fifty. Understand?"

"Yes, sir. I won't let you down."

Maya saluted the officers and rushed back to join her friends, grateful she had dodged a bullet. This time.

CHAPTER TEN

Six weeks later

MANGERIAN SAT BEHIND her desk, working her way through a seemingly never-ending stack of emails that needed to be read, legislature that needed to be signed, and a ton of other stuff that needed to be attended to. Everyone thought being Governor was the easiest job in USC7, nothing but attending ceremonies, giving speeches, and kissing babies, although there were few of the latter due to strict population control policies. Only a few realized that stuff made the job sane. Like everyone else in the facility, the Governor worked five days a week, more often seven, to make sure the facility functioned properly for the survival of everyone. Granted, she did not perform her duties in the stench and grime of the sub-basements, but that did not mean her hands were clean. Every leader throughout history had been faced with the moral dilemma of choosing between what was right and what was best for the greater good. Mangerian had spent many a sleepless night struggling with some of the decisions she had made during her administration.

If she won tomorrow's election, she would have that much more to add to her anxiety.

Mangerian had sent her staff home early since tomorrow promised to be a hectic day, no matter the outcome. However, it did not surprise her when a knock sounded on her door.

"Come in. It's open."

Devon stepped in. "I'm sorry I'm late. I had another meeting and didn't want to appear suspicious by leaving early."

"That's all right, Devon. Have a seat."

He sat in one of the wing-backed chairs in front of the Governor. "Is everything okay, Madam Governor? You seem frustrated."

Mangerian held up the report she had been reading then tossed it on top of the pile. "One of the hydroponic units broke down. Maintenance says it'll take a week to repair. They jury-rigged a second system that's about to fail, but it's not that effective. We may lose one percent of our crops for this cycle."

"That's not going to go over well with the citizens."

"Under the circumstances, they're lucky to be living so well. I'll bullshit my way out of it like I do with every bit of bad news." She leaned back in her chair. "Are we all set for the elections?"

"Yes, ma'am. I've assigned at least two reliable persons to every polling station in New Quincy. General Arasaki assures me the same is true with the other sectors. Everything will run smoothly."

"Good. I knew I could count on you."

"Thank you, Madam Governor."

"I'd like to assign Maya to the team at your polling station."

Devon's eyes lit up at the prospect of seeing his girlfriend, but he maintained his professional composure. "Isn't that a bit unusual, ma'am? I mean, using cadets and EDF personnel for polling station duty?"

"It is, but she's an exception. Denning told me she's the top-ranking cadet in her class. She's going to be an asset to the defense forces. I'd like to think we can someday bring her into the inner circle."

"I'll talk to Colonel Denning in the morning and see if he'll agree to transfer her for the day. They've almost completed their training."

"Thank you, Devon. I knew I could count on you." The Governor's demeanor relaxed. "You did well pushing for Maya to be a cadet."

"Thank you, ma'am. But I only recommended her."

"Don't be modest. I've been playing this game too long. You dropped ear worms about her with the right people. I even know you overlooked that indiscretion Hall got herself in, so she would recommend Maya to the legislative council."

Devon's expression changed to one of shock. To his credit, he did not attempt to deny the allegations. "I'm sorry about that, ma'am. Given the situation—"

Mangerian cut him off. "No need to apologize. You broke the rules, but sometimes you need to for the greater good. Besides, it never hurts to have a few politicians in your corner who owe you a favor."

Devon exhaled audibly. "I'm glad you're not mad."

"You did well. If I win, I'm going to open slots for cadets to Ring D citizens. Keep it up, and soon you'll be sitting in this chair."

"Thank you, Madam Governor."

A grin pierced Mangerian's lips, both humorous and frustrated "You won't thank me once you get into this office. Keep me apprised of the situation tomorrow. Dismissed."

Devon stood at attention, saluted, and left.

Mangerian went back to her business, hoping tomorrow went as planned.

CHAPTER ELEVEN

OVER THE PAST seven weeks, the cadets had fallen into a routine. Reveille, dress in fatigues, chow hall, and then report to the gym. They expected some form of physical torture such as twenty laps with full backpacks. Instead, the shooting range had been set up again. Only this time, paper targets were mounted on a thickly cushioned backdrop one hundred feet from the shooting line, and their weapons, along with considerable ammunition, replaced the paintball guns.

Byrd stood by the shooting line. "Come on, people. We don't have all day."

The cadets double-timed over, excited about training on real weapons.

Then Bodman nudged Sanchez and whispered, "We get to play with the real guns today."

Maya cringed, knowing what would happen next.

Byrd appeared in front of Bodman as if he had been teleported. He shoved his face against Bodman's and launched into his tirade.

"Did you just say, 'play with guns,' Porky?"

"Y-yes, sir."

"Do you think this is a game?"

"No, sir."

"We don't *play*. We train. And they're not guns. They're lethal weapons of war. Do you understand?"

"Yes, sir."

"I don't think you do." Byrd paced along the cadets. "I don't think any of you do. Grab your M4s and fall in line."

What fresh hell is this? thought Maya. She picked up her Carnie, remembering to pull back the slide and check the barrel for any rounds. The others followed her example, thankful she had remembered. No one wanted more abuse.

A few minutes later, the cadets began the first of ten laps around the gym led by Byrd. Each held a Carbine in their right hand, the barrel resting on their shoulder, and clutched their crotch with the other. They raised or grabbed their Carbines or crotches, respectively, to the chant, "This is my weapon. This is my gun. This is for fighting. This is for fun."

When the cadets had learned their lesson and returned to the firing range, Byrd made an announcement.

"Listen up, sewer roaches. I have a surprise for you. You won't have to put up with my charming personality for a while. It's Election Day. For the remainder of the day, you'll each be assigned to a separate polling station to oversee our glorious election process and observe first-hand what you will be fighting to defend. It'll be a good experience for you. I have your assignments here. Once you receive them, take a shower, get into your dress uniforms, and be sure to report to your assigned station at 0930."

Byrd handed out the assignments. Maya received hers last.

"You've been assigned NQ3127 Ring D. Meet Lieutenant Williams there. He'll brief you on what you need to do. Dismissed."

Maya almost skipped back to the barracks, more excited about seeing Devon than the particular assignment.

✧   ✧   ✧

WHEN MAYA ARRIVED at NQ3127 Ring D at 0920, a line of voters had already formed along the corridor waiting for voting to begin. An IDF private stood at the door. He nodded as Maya entered.

The gymnasium for New Quincy High School had been

temporarily converted into the polling station. The staff had pushed the bleachers and sports equipment against one wall. Two desks sat near the entrance, one to check IDs and another to issue ballots. Along two walls of the gym stood curtained voting booths. The ballot box sat in the center, overseen by a man and a woman, both in civilian clothes. Maya smiled when she saw Devon standing in the corner talking to one of the officials.

She went over and stood ten feet away. When Devon finished, he turned to her.

Maya snapped to attention and saluted. "Cadet Santos reporting as ordered, sir."

"At ease." Then, in a whisper. "It's good to see you, hon."

"Likewise. Did you recommend me for this?"

"The Governor did. She's impressed with your training and wanted you to get the experience. Luckily, she assigned you to me."

"I'm glad she did."

"Follow me. I'll show you what you have to do," Devon said in a loud and assertive voice for the benefit of the civilians.

They walked over to the desk reserved for the IDF. "The job is simple. We merely oversee the process to ensure election integrity. Two candidates, one chosen by each party, man the ballot box. Other representatives from the two parties will be here throughout the day to make sure things run smoothly."

Devon handed her a clipboard with blank paper attached to it. "If there are any disputes, we listen in and take notes, marking the time and the details of the dispute. Don't say anything and don't get involved. At the end of the voting, our notes will be sent to the election commission. Other than that, try not to die of boredom."

"Do we get any breaks?" Maya made no effort to hide the innuendo in her tone.

"Cadet, you're on assignment, and fraternization during business hours is forbidden."

"Yes, sir," Maya said with a sense of deflation.

"However," Devon lowered his voice. "Once the ballots are passed to the election commission for counting, I'll have time to give you an evaluation of your performance." He winked.

"Yes, sir."

✧　✧　✧

THE POLLS OPENED at 1000. The process went exactly as Maya had learned in Civics, only far more monotonous. All day, voters came in, cast their ballots, then left. No issues occurred. The few times that Maya and Devon got to chat involved mundane stuff, mostly about her training. Devon offered advice and warned her what not to do to piss off Byrd.

At 1930, the officials who would tally the votes arrived, ten from each party.

The polls closed promptly at 2000. The officials set to work counting the votes. One would count the ballots while the official from the other party would verify it. Maya and Devon stood on either end of the rows of tables overseeing the process.

Vote counting concluded a little after 2100 and the results announced – 53.1 percent for Riviera and 48.9 for Mangerian. The election staff placed the ballots and results in a white box and closed the lid with packing tape. Each election official signed their name to the tape, followed by Maya and Devon and the head of the polling station, who then placed the box on a cart.

"Now what?" asked Maya.

"We take it to the Office of the Election Commission. Once the officials here receive word that it's been delivered, they'll head home. Are you ready?"

"Yes, sir."

Devon pushed the cart out of the polling station and headed toward Ring C. Maya walked beside him. Neither spoke, maintaining a professional air.

"Where are we heading?"

"NS989 in Ring C."

Devon stopped at the interconnecting corridor between New Quincy and New Salem, scanned the area to make sure no one was around, and then diverted back toward Ring D.

"What are you doing?"

"Trust me, and don't say anything."

"But aren't we—"

"That's an order from your commanding officer."

Maya did not know if she felt more hurt or scared by Devon's tone.

Devon stopped at the first door on the left. The sign on the door read GARBAGE DISPOSAL: 0600 TO 1000. He knocked twice, paused, then knocked again. The door opened. An IDF non-comm reached out and took the ballot box. A moment later, a second IDF non-comm reached through and placed an exact replica of the one removed, including the twenty-three names written on the tape. Maya stepped forward to peer inside. As the door closed, she spotted the first IDF non-comm dropping the original box into a metal drum containing a fire. The flames intensified as the box ignited.

Devon had already returned to the Ring C corridor. "What are you waiting for?"

Maya hesitated.

"Move it, cadet."

She fell in beside Devon. Neither spoke nor made eye contact.

They reached the Office of the Election Commission a few minutes later. Two IDF officers stood guard out front. The one on the left opened the door, closing it behind them once they entered.

Nearly one hundred desks sat around the room, each holding two people. Most opened the returned ballot boxes and counted the ballots, making sure they matched the poll count included on the slip of paper inside.

Devon wheeled the cart over to a table near the entrance. "I have the results from New Quincy Polling Station C."

"Thank you." A middle-aged woman with dark hair took the box. She checked the names on the side of the box and cross-checked them with a list on her desk. "Are you Lieutenant Devon Williams?"

"I am."

"Do you certify that this box has not left your sight or been tampered with since leaving New Quincy Polling Station C?"

"I do."

The woman focused her attention on Maya. "Are you Cadet Santos?

"I am."

"Do you certify that this box has not left your sight or been tampered with since leaving New Quincy Polling Station C?"

A knot formed in the pit of Maya's stomach. She had been raised never to lie, but she had also been raised never to disobey orders. Reluctantly, she replied, "I do."

The woman picked up a phone and placed a call. It rang twice.

"Is this Nathan Johnson at New Quincy Polling Station C?"

"It is."

"This is Martha of the Office of the Election Commission. Your ballot box has arrived and is certified as legitimate."

"Thank you."

The woman nodded to a man in his earlier twenties who came around the front of the table. He signed his name to the tape beneath Johnson's and then took the box to a table where two election officials also signed the tape and cut the seal. One of the officials removed the paper, studied it, and passed it to his counterpart. The latter called out, "New Quincy Polling Station C. The results are 48.7 percent for Riviera and 51.3 percent for Mangerian."

What the hell is going on? Maya asked herself, although she knew the answer.

The woman turned to Maya and Devon. "Thank you both. You're dismissed."

Once out in the corridor and away from the other IDF officers, Maya asked, "What just went on back there?"

"I'll explain later. Don't talk about this to anyone." Devon's tone was not a lover to another but a commanding officer issuing an order to a subordinate.

Maya felt nauseous.

"Come on. We can watch the results in the IDF lounge." This time Devon spoke more lovingly. "I'll buy you a drink."

✧   ✧   ✧

MAYA DID NOT feel like socializing but, under the circumstances, thought it better to be around others until this charade ended. True to his word, Devon bought her a drink, a tumbler half-filled with whiskey made from a distillery in Ring E. She nursed it along, not enjoying the taste. She did not want anything right now and preferred to sit at a table in the corner by herself, not caring that Devon abandoned her to be with his fellow officers.

Shortly after midnight, the local TV monitor announced the election results were in and would be aired in a few minutes. Everyone except Maya gathered around. Riviera: 49.1. Mangerian: 50.9. Mangerian would serve a fourth term as Governor of USC7.

Most of the IDF personnel cheered and patted each other on the back. Those who supported Riviera quietly left the lounge, dejected.

Devon wandered over to Maya's table. "Now, how about that evaluation of your performance?"

The last thing Maya wanted right now was to be intimate. She did not even want to be around Devon. Maya stood and headed for the exit. "Sorry, but I'm exhausted and have to get up early tomorrow."

Devon stepped in front of her. "Are you okay?"

"Yes," she lied. "I have to get going. And don't worry, I won't say anything about today."

Maya stormed out of the lounge and made her way back to the barracks. She quietly dressed in her skivvies so as not to disturb the other cadets and slid into her bunk.

Sleep did not come easily. Maya tossed and turned in her bunk, trying to grasp what she had witnessed and not being able to come to terms with her part in it. They had rigged the election results. Those few seconds in front of the garbage disposal room dashed everything she had been taught and believed about democracy and integrity in USC7. What else about the facility was a sham? The IDF, supposedly neutral and above board, had rigged this election. Did they do it on their own? Or worse, did they do it at the behest of the Governor? What other lies were being kept from the citizens? For the first time in her life, Maya questioned the ideal that she once held about USC7 and her moral compass.

Even worse, what about Devon? He seemed to be doing this willingly. That was not the man she had fallen in love with. What compelled him to break the rules he was sworn to uphold? Hell, did he even care for her, or was their relationship merely a means to bring her into the corruption? At this moment, she never wanted to see him again.

She did not even want to confront herself in the mirror.

Maya's thoughts and emotions churned inside her until exhaustion eventually took over and she fell asleep. She dozed for less than two hours when reveille erupted over the loudspeakers.

CHAPTER TWELVE

R AT TRAP LAY on the frozen snow, partially hidden behind a snowdrift. The sun had gone down several hours ago, sparing him the blinding glare of its rays reflecting off the surface. On the downside, the night temperature dropped thirty degrees until he felt the cold biting through his thermal suit. It had to be at least negative forty. He ignored it, focusing his attention on the mission at hand. Peering through his night vision binoculars, he watched the Hagglund from USC7 make its rounds around the facility's perimeter.

His team had been stuck out in here in the tundra near USC7 for close to three weeks, observing the patrol schedule of the EDF. Despite the dangers and hardships, their vigil had paid off. Rat Trap had found a vulnerability in their defenses that left the facility open to invasion.

Not facing a clear and present danger, USC7's security detail had fallen into a routine. The EDF broke down the exterior patrols into six four-hour shifts, which made sense, but those shifts ran like clockwork. Three Hagglunds emerged from the elevator within ten minutes of the beginning of the shift and then proceeded on their patrols. Inevitably, they all returned within fifteen minutes of the end of their shift and waited for their replacements to arrive. The EDF stationed only two guards inside the elevator bay, with the doors closed during patrols. That gave them a three-and-a-half-hour window to launch their invasion, a task made much easier thanks to the uniforms and IDs the previous team had taken from the patrol ambushed six weeks ago.

That operation had been a risk, but one worth taking. The Hagglund happened to pass near the team while they were conducting reconnaissance. The team commander ordered his men to sneak up on the vehicle and take down the crew, which turned out to be much easier than expected. They stripped the bodies of their uniforms, IDs, and weapons, then executed them and left the bodies for the polar bears. The biggest take had been the radios because now they could listen in on EDF communications. The dumb bastards never thought to change frequencies, allowing the marauders to gather a wealth of intelligence, all of which they radioed back to the Boss. They ransacked the Hagglund, mainly to take it out of commission but partly to let the EDF think the attack had been by one of the groups of marauders that still roamed the country.

Rat Trap waited until the midnight shift returned to the elevator and the next shift appeared, both within the twenty-five-minute time frame. Once the area cleared out, he made his way back to camp.

Camp was an underground cave formed in the ice two miles from USC7. His team had been lucky to discover it. Though cold and cramped—the cave had an oval shape twenty-plus feet long and only half as wide, with a five-foot headspace—it saved them from having to set up tents above ground, which exposed them to the elements. After three weeks of living there, the cave was humid and stank of sweat. Ducking low, he entered.

Charlie sat at a makeshift table made from a box of supplies. He jumped on hearing Rat Trap, grabbed his Carbine, and aimed it at his buddy. After a second, he lowered the weapon.

"God damn. Fucking warn us next time you come in."

"Relax. It's only me."

"I almost killed you. I thought you were a bear."

Rat Trap removed his sunglasses and hat then tossed them on the table. "Don't be so jittery."

"Do you blame him?" asked Jimmy Benedetto from his sleeping bag where he lay spread out. "Anyone would be trigger happy after three weeks in this shithole."

"We have all the information we need," added Charlie. "Can't we get out of here now?"

"The Boss told us to stay here three weeks. You want to disobey him?"

"No," Charlie replied sullenly.

"Besides, we only have two days left, then we go home. Nut up."

Rat Trap sat on his sleeping nag, his legs crossed beneath him, and pulled the two-way radio close. Switching it on, he dialed the correct frequency and pressed the talk button on the microphone.

"Delta Team to base. Do you read me?"

A moment of silence passed before a familiar voice responded. "I hear you, Delta Team. Hang on while I get the Boss."

A few minutes later, the Boss' voice came over the radio. "Everything okay?"

"Yup. This is just a normal check-in. The EDF teams are still following the same procedures as before. No change, even after the ambush."

"That's good to know. They have no idea what's about to happen."

"It seems that way."

"Your guy arrived yesterday with the IDs. Excellent job."

"Thank you." Rat Trap beamed. "Do you want us to continue the mission or return home?"

"It's only two more days, so stay put. Your replacements are on their way."

"Roger that. We'll be here when they show up."

The radio went dead. Rat Trap placed the microphone on its clip and pushed the radio aside. "I tried."

"Thanks." Jimmy pulled the wool cap over his eyes and

went back to sleep.

"I'm going to grab some sleep, too," said Charlie.

"No problem. I'm too wound up to rest. I'll wake you in an hour to stand guard."

Rat Trap opened his backpack, removed a small can of processed meat, tore off the lid, and ate with a tarnished spoon. The meat tasted like shit, but at least it satisfied his hunger. He never asked what the cooks put in it. Considering the rats and roaches that overran their facility, he didn't want to know. Not that it mattered. Soon he would be sleeping in a warm, comfortable bed and dining on real food.

CHAPTER THIRTEEN

MAYA STOOD AT attention in the gymnasium, her excitement over training replaced by a melancholy feeling over what had happened last night. She thought their training had been to prepare them to defend USC7 and democracy, not subvert it.

Her heart skipped a beat when Captain Haskell, the First Shift CO, entered and made his way over to Byrd.

"This is your lucky day, sewer roaches," announced Byrd. "Since your training is almost over and you've proven yourselves capable of minimal defense force skills, Captain Haskell has requested you all do a stint topside."

A flurry of excitement went through the cadets. Maya almost clapped her hands in joy. She would finally get to see Above Earth.

"Settle down," admonished Byrd. "Cadets Santos and Daniels will go out with the next shift, followed by Butterfingers and Carver at 1200, Porky and Barbie at 1600, and Arasaki and Sanchez at 2000. When you're not topside getting a dose of reality, you'll be down here conducting weapons training with me. Is that clear?"

"Sir, yes, sir."

Haskell stepped forward. "Cadets Santos and Daniels, you're with me."

The two women broke ranks and followed Haskell into the corridor. They made their way to the lowest level of the sub-basements. The inner wall of Ring A contained two large bay doors. Both were open. Maya's eyes widened when they entered.

The area enclosed by Ring A housed a giant elevator shaft measuring a thousand feet across. Three elevator pads large enough to hold a Hagglund sat against the walls, two on the left side of the bay doors and one on the right. The fifth wall contained a line of forty lockers. Thirteen EDF soldiers stood in front of them in various stages of undress. Haskell headed toward them.

"This is Cadet Santos and Cadet Daniels. They'll be accompanying us to observe today's recon."

The others acknowledged with grunts and waves.

"Your gear is in lockers twelve and thirteen."

Maya and Bettany stripped out of their fatigues and boots. Each locker contained sports underwear, a woolen base layer to control moisture and provide additional warmth, a lightweight nylon shirt and trousers, a fleece insulation layer, a down core jacket with a fur-lined hood, fleece insulated outer trousers, waterproof all-weather boots and thermal socks, a wool beanie, category four sunglasses, wool inner gloves, and fleece-lined abrasion-resistant outer gloves.

When she finished dressing, Maya felt like a tick about to burst. A restricted, sweating tick. She roasted inside the cold-weather gear.

"Did we do this right?" asked Bettany. "The others have full freedom of movement."

Maya shrugged. "Maybe they're used to it."

After the soldiers performed the mandatory checks on their weapons and were loaded and locked, Haskell maneuvered himself in front of the lockers. "Fall in."

The soldiers obeyed, with Maya and Bettany at the end of the formation.

"SOP today. Look for signs of marauders. Try to avoid polar bears. Stay safe and stay frosty."

"That won't be difficult, sir," responded a lieutenant.

The rest of the soldiers responded with, "Hooah."

"Dismissed." As the others broke off and headed for the respective vehicles, Haskell walked past Maya and Bettany. "Daniels, you go with Badau. Santos, you're with me."

Haskell took the passenger seat while Maya climbed in back. Haskell gave a thumbs-up through the window. A sergeant standing near the edge of the elevator responded in kind and pressed a button on his console. The elevator began to rise.

Haskell shifted in his seat to look at Maya. He pointed to the driver and the other soldier in back. "This is Sergeant Kim and Corporal Thomson. We're on a routine mission. Do what we tell you to and you'll be fine. For now, relax and enjoy your first trip to Above Earth."

That was the best order Maya had been given since entering basic training. She fidgeted in her seat as the elevator made its slow, five-minute ascent to the surface.

An exceptionally bright light reflected off the wall. Maya glanced out the window. A hundred feet above her, a roof braced by dozens of heavy support beams blocked her view. The light came from the three openings for the elevators. It became more intense the closer they got. As the platform passed through its slot, the light became so intense Maya had to close her eyes. It took a minute for her vision to adjust.

Haskell stepped out onto the platform. A frigid burst of air flowed into the cab. Maya shivered. The leader of each Hagglund team met their returning counterparts, chatted briefly, and returned to their vehicles. Maya braced for the burst of cold air that filled the cab, although now she knew what to expect.

Haskell closed the door behind him. "Nothing unusual to report. Let's head out."

Kim exited the bay, proceeding up a snow ramp to the surface. The light blinded Maya. She winced.

"Put your sunglasses on," advised Thompson. "It'll help you see better. It's also for your safety. If you don't wear them, the light reflecting off the surface can cause snow blindness."

"Thanks, corporal."

"Call me Dorrie."

Maya slid the sunglasses over her eyes. The view had a bluish-black tint, but it did nothing to detract from the magnificent vista spread out around her. She had seen photos of this all her life. However, none of them compared to reality.

Snow stretched as far as the horizon, the flat landscape occasionally broken by drifts of various shapes and sizes. The wind blew across the surface, churning the loose snow into mini tornados of white that spun wildly in the air before settling back to earth. The gusts slammed against the windows and rocked the Hagglund. Maya never imagined Above Earth would be so breathtaking.

Once out of the bay, Kim turned right and drove along the facility's perimeter past a small mountain of ice.

"What are we doing?"

Haskell shifted in his seat to face her. "The search grid is divided into three sectors. Each team checks their section of the perimeter for damage before moving inland. It's SOP."

Snow covered the dome of the upper elevator bay to a height of nearly a hundred feet. They drove for several thousand feet before coming across an ice tunnel that sloped down toward the facility.

"What's that?"

"The emergency exit in case the elevators fail. It's a stairwell that leads to the lowest sub-basement. It's not bad going down but coming up is a nightmare."

With the perimeter check completed, Kim veered left and headed out into the tundra. Maya stared out, fascinated by what she saw.

"Impressive, isn't it?" asked Haskell.

"I've never seen anything so beautiful in my life."

"I remember my first time on Above Earth. The landscape is enthralling. Over time, you'll learn that it's as dangerous as it is mesmerizing."

Maya pointed to the right where two tall structures stood above the horizon. "What are those?"

Haskell looked out the window. "That's Boston. Most of the city is buried under snow and ice. Those are the Prudential Building and I can't remember the name of the other one."

"I think it's the Hanson Building, sir," said Kim.

"Hancock Building," corrected Dorrie.

"Has anyone been there?" asked Maya.

"A few patrols were sent there during the first year to search for survivors but found nothing. No one has been there since. The stories they brought back are still told among the EDF."

Kim chuckled. "Though somewhat exaggerated."

"It's a soldier's right to embellish, corporal."

Maya stared at the skyline until it disappeared. A city buried under snow and ice. Streets, homes, businesses, schools, libraries, perfectly preserved for future archaeologists to discover. Her mind raced with unanswered questions. How much history of the Old World had been preserved? Did the ice capture these cities in their pristine glory as in Egypt or the chaos of their last moments as in Pompeii? How many bodies lay within that frozen tomb? Maya found the concepts both fascinating and disturbing. She someday wanted to visit one of these cities and see it firsthand.

Three hours into their mission, while heading back to USC7, Kim pointed ahead of him. "Looks like we found an ice cave."

"What does that mean?" Maya asked Dorrie.

"There's probably polar bears in it. They've been attacking us a lot lately. We make nice, warm snacks."

"Are we going in after them?"

"No," answered Haskell. "We'll flush them out. Park a hundred feet from the entrance."

Kim pulled up and shut down the engine.

"Okay, people. Safeties off. Kill anything that comes out."

They opened the doors and climbed out. Having gotten used to the heat inside the cab, Maya winced when the biting cold cut through her. She shivered despite her parka and thermal underwear. Ignoring the conditions, she focused on the mission, not wanting to screw up her first time out.

Haskell stopped Maya and Dorrie fifty feet from the cave entrance. They provided cover as Kim snuck forward, pulled the pin on a tear gas canister, and lobbed it through the opening. The sergeant raced back. Before he could rejoin the others, gunfire erupted from inside the cave. A figure ran out, tears flowing from his eyes. He brandished a Carbine and fired it indiscriminately. None of the bullets were even close to hitting their target. However, he still posed a danger to the team.

Maya fired a quick burst, all three rounds catching the figure in his chest. He fell face-first into the mound, his skull fracturing as it hit the frozen snow. Blood flowed from the wounds, creating wisps of steam on the ice.

"I want the others alive," yelled Haskell as he surged toward the cave.

A second figure stumbled out, his eyes closed, his hands reaching out in front of him like a blind man. He did not have a weapon. Haskell ran up and slammed the stock of his Carbine into the man's abdomen. He dropped to his knees and doubled over in pain. Haskell then hit the man on the side of his head, not hard enough to knock him unconscious but to stun him. Kim and Dorrie secured his ankles and wrists with plastic ties.

A third figure emerged, this one brandishing a knife and screaming. He could not see due to the tear gas and attacked the first blur that caught his vision, which happened to be Haskell. With his back to the attacker, the captain could not defend himself.

Maya fired three rounds at the attacker's legs. The third

caught him in the left shin, shattering the bone. He dropped onto the ice, still screaming, only this time in pain. Haskell spun around and saw the man lying three feet from him, still clutching the knife. The captain placed his boot on the attacker's right wrist, preventing him from using the blade, then slammed the Carbine's stock into the side of his head, rendering him unconscious.

Kim rushed over to check on them. "Do you want me to see if there are any more inside?"

Haskell shook his head. "Too much tear gas. Fire into the cave. That'll flush out anyone still inside or eliminate the threat."

Kim fired three short bursts into the cave. Only the sounds of bullets ricocheting off the ice came from inside.

"Sergeant, bag and tag this one, then leave Thompson to guard them. Call headquarters and tell them what we found. Have them send out two teams, one to take the prisoners back for questioning and one with gas masks to search the cave."

"Yes, sir."

Once the prisoners were secured, Dorrie stood guard as Kim returned to the Hagglund to call in.

Haskell stepped over to Maya. "Why didn't you kill that third attacker when he came after me?"

"I'm sorry, sir." Maya prepared for a major dressing down. "You said you wanted them taken alive."

"Don't worry, cadet. You're not in trouble. You did what I told you to."

Maya realized her brow sweated despite the sub-zero temperature. "Are these the marauders everyone has been mentioning?"

"No." The captain's military professionalism momentarily faded. "I hoped you'd complete training before I had to tell you."

Curiosity overwhelmed Maya. "Tell me what?"

"USC7 is not the only facility out here."

CHAPTER FOURTEEN

ONCE BACK AT USC7, Haskell requested that Maya be allowed to sit in on the interrogation of the prisoners since she had been part of the capture. Denning granted permission. After changing back into their fatigues, Haskell led her to a room on Ring A where everything from the cave and the prisoners' clothes and personal belongings were laid out on tables. To Maya's surprise, she found Devon examining the items.

"What are you doing here?" she asked.

Haskell answered. "Lieutenant Williams is an intelligence officer for the defense forces."

Devon looked at her and smiled. Damn, how many secrets did the bastard keep from her?

"What did you find?" asked Haskell.

"Not much, sir." Devon motioned them over to have a look for themselves.

Nothing seemed unusual. Three sleeping bags. Boxes of canned foods, although from their appearance they were not as good as those from their facility. Six Carbines, three of them much more weathered than the ones they used, plus three M17s and Ka-Bar knifes in good condition. Their clothes were identical to the EDF uniforms, and the cold-weather gear looked the same except for the USC5 patches on the shoulders. Rather than fatigues, the prisoners wore civilian clothing and t-shirts, all of them dirty and tattered. The only item that caught Maya's attention was the two-way radio in the middle of one of the tables.

"I found two things of interest. The first is their radio."

"Do we know what frequency they use?" asked Haskell.

"Not yet, sir. These guys practiced good OPSEC." Devon glanced over at Maya. "That's operational security." He turned his attention back to the captain. "When finished, they change the settings. Given time, my people will figure it out. There's also this."

Devon handed Haskell a notebook. The captain thumbed through it.

"Damn, they've been observing our patrols and noting the times."

"Yes, sir. They've been doing that for almost three weeks."

"Three weeks?"

Devon nodded. "I think these people, or a team before them, killed our patrol six weeks ago. Three of the Carbines, the M17s, and the knives belong to the team they ambushed."

"What about our people's clothes and IDs?"

"I haven't found them. I assume they were already sent back."

"Fuck." Haskell stepped away from the table, running the different scenarios through his head. "I'll tell Denning to increase the patrols and add an extra person to each team. We'll also stagger the patrol times."

"I'd also recommend increasing the guard on both levels of the elevator shaft and conducting security checks of every patrol when they get back."

"Done. Any info on the prisoners?"

"Just the one killed." Devon handed the captain a photograph with a bullet hole through it. Dried blood stained the image. "His name was Charlie. At least that was the name written on the back of a photo he carried. He had a wife and two kids. I found no identification for the others."

"Have you interrogated them yet?"

"No, sir. I thought you and Colonel Denning would want to be present for that."

"Good call. When do you want to do it?"

"As soon as possible while they're still scared and confused."

"I'll have them ready in fifteen minutes. What do you need?"

"Four guards. I'll bring everything else." Devon paused. "I'd also like Cadet Santos there to observe."

"Consider it done. Cadet, you're with me."

Haskell exited the room with Maya behind him. She had dozens of questions but said nothing, hoping everything would fall into place during the interrogation.

✧   ✧   ✧

RAT TRAP AND Jimmy sat in metal chairs in front of a steel table. The guards who had brought them in put metal clamps welded to the legs of the chairs around their ankles and secured their wrists to another set of clamps on the table's surface, then left them alone. None of them spoke as they transferred the prisoners from their cells, part of the intimidation process. Rat Trap knew the procedure by heart. Both men were hunched forward, unable to rest their backs on the seats, and wore only sweatpants and t-shirts.

After they had been alone a few minutes, Rat Trap whispered to Jimmy, "Don't tell them anything."

"What if they torture us?"

"They're not going to torture us. They'll just try to scare you into talking. And that's the last thing you want to do."

"Why?"

Rat Trap growled his answer. "This place will be ours in a few weeks. Do you want the Boss to waltz in here and find out you ratted him out?"

"No." Jimmy blanched at the thought of what the Boss would do to him.

"Exactly. See that mirror off to the left?"

"Yeah."

"It's a two-way mirror. The defense forces are watching us from the other side. Don't give these assholes any satisfaction. Tell them nothing and give them shit. We'll be fine in the long run."

✦   ✦   ✦

MAYA, DEVON, DENNING, and Haskell stood on the opposite side of the mirror, studying the prisoners.

"Cadet Santos," asked Devon. "What's your assessment?"

"The one with the beard is the boss. He's tough and arrogant. You'll have a difficult time getting him to talk."

"I don't intend to. The other one is practically pissing his pants already. He's the one I want to break." Devon turned his attention to Haskell. "Are we ready, sir?"

"Whenever you are."

"Cadet, you're with me."

Devon headed for the door, pausing long enough to pick up a baseball bat resting against the jamb. Maya paused, uncertain about what would happen next.

Four IDF guards waited outside the interrogation room. Devon handed the baseball bat to the tallest one. "You four will stay in the back of the room. You know what to do."

"Yes, sir," each replied.

Devon turned to Maya. "You're up front with me. Remember, you're only here to observe. Don't say or do anything unless I tell you to. Is that clear?"

"Yes, sir." She replied with no emotion.

"Let's do this."

Devon entered the interrogation room. Maya stayed close. The four guards stood behind the prisoners. The frightened one glanced over his shoulder and broke into a sweat. Devon positioned himself in front of the table. Maya stood two yards behind and to his left.

"I'm not telling you nothing," spat Rat Trap. "So don't waste your time."

"I'm not going to." Devon bent over and rested his hands on the table. "We have your notes and know you're planning an assault on the facility. It'll save us both a lot of time and effort if you tell me everything you know."

"Go fuck yourself."

"Suit yourself."

Devon began to leave. Maya watched, dumbstruck. These past few days, she had come to know Devon as an enigma. But she never expected him to give up so—

Devon stopped by the tallest guard, took the baseball bat, and spun around to Rat Trap. He landed the first strike on the prisoner's right shoulder blade. The sound of bones shattering could be heard even over Rat Trap's cry. Devon brought the bat down again on the same spot. Rat Trap screamed. The ball joint dislocated from its socket, leaving his arm hanging limp. Devon switched his attention to the left shoulder with the same results. The fifth and final blow fell across his back. Rat Trap collapsed on the table, unconscious.

Maya swallowed the vomit rising in her throat.

Devon pointed to the tallest guard. "Take him out and leave him where we found him. Either his people or the polar bears will find him."

Two guards stepped forward. One held Rat Trap in place as the other unlocked the restraints. Once free, they took Rat Trap under each shoulder and dragged him away. The third guard opened the door and let them out, closing it behind them and resuming his position behind Jimmy.

Maya smelled urine and feces. Jimmy had soiled himself. A pool of piss formed at his feet.

Devon sat on the edge of the table beside Jimmy. He held the handle of the bat in his hands with the end resting on the floor. "As you can see, I'm not fucking around. Your friend got off easy. You won't be as lucky."

Jimmy's eyes focused on the bat. "P-please, d-don't hurt me."

"I won't if you tell me what you know."

Jimmy remained silent.

"You do know something, I assume."

"Y-yes."

"Then tell me."

Jimmy focused his gaze on the bat. It didn't matter. Whatever this guy put him through would be nothing compared with what the Boss would do to him if the Boss ever found out he talked.

"I can't."

"Too bad." Devon nodded to the guards.

One of them stepped forward. Jimmy closed his eyes and winced, waiting to be pummeled with the bat. Instead, the guard removed a hypodermic from his pocket, pulled off the cap, plunged the needle into the back of Jimmy's neck, and pushed the plunger. Jimmy went limp in the chair.

Maya fought down another round of vomitus. "Is he dead?"

"Just unconscious. We gave him a powerful sedative." Devon motioned toward Jimmy. "Take him to IDF med bay."

The two guards unlocked Jimmy and dragged him away. A moment later, Denning and Haskell entered.

"What now?" asked the captain.

"I'll use enhanced interrogation techniques. He'll talk soon enough."

"Good. Use any methods you feel are necessary, only don't inform me about them."

"Same here," added Haskell.

"Don't worry, sirs. You'll have culpable deniability."

Devon saluted, and both men departed, leaving Devon and Maya alone.

"Who are you?" asked Maya, aghast.

"What do you mean?"

"The way you brutalized that first prisoner. And what do you mean by enhanced interrogation techniques?"

"You don't want to know."

"You're right. I don't." Maya chose her next words carefully. "I don't know who you are anymore."

"I'm the same person you fell in love with and who's in love with you."

Maya felt as if she had been struck by the bat. "I can't believe the first time you tell me you love me is after I watch you torture a man to death."

Devon softened his tone. "I do love you. And I trust and respect you. That's why I recommended you for the EDF."

"I could never do what you just did."

"Stop comparing me to my job. I have to be harsh to protect the facility."

"Two people died today!"

"If I recall, you killed one of them yourself."

Maya got into Devon's face. "Don't you play those bullshit games with me. That was self-defense. I didn't know they're marauders looking for food."

Devon laughed derisively, which infuriated her even more.

"I'm glad you find me amusing."

"Maya, you're one of the smartest people I know, but you're as naïve as a baby." He reached up and pulled the sleeve of his shirt so the emblem faced her. "Didn't you ever wonder why these are labeled USC *Seven?* Did you even notice that the uniforms we took from the prisoners read USC *Five?*"

Maya's rage drained away as the realization slowly dawned on her.

Devon placed a comforting hand on her shoulder. "We're not alone out here."

"How many...?" Maya stumbled to find the right words.

"We built almost a thousand facilities, all of them the same design as this one. The original idea was to save two million people in the hopes that, if the Great Freeze ever ended, we'd have a chance of re-populating the planet. It turned out to be a pipedream."

"What happened?"

"At first, every the facilities worked together. The citizens adapted to their new environments. Everything went as planned. Shortly after our first anniversary underground, the whole concept became a Charlie Foxtrot. USC13 out in Colorado experienced a meltdown of one of their nuclear reactors. Half the facility left and died of exposure. The half that stayed slowly died of radiation poisoning. USC27 in London had its livestock wiped out by mad cow disease. The hydroponic units in several others failed. Riots broke out, the citizens killing each other for food. Idiots ran some of the other facilities who drove their facilities into the ground. Revolutions took place in others, setting up dictatorships. The facilities in Russia and China abandoned democracy for Communism. Many suffered from communication failures and dropped off the grid. By the end of the second year, most of the facilities failed or devolved into anarchy. By the end of the third year, we stopped communicating with the other facilities so others wouldn't try to take what we had."

"Are we the only facility left?"

Devon sat on the edge of the table. "No. As far as we know, we're one of the few, if not the only facility, that survived intact. USC5 is in New York near Albany. About eight months ago, they found out about us and have been spying on and harassing us. Intelligence assesses that an attack on USC7 is imminent."

It all fell into place for Maya. "We rigged the election because Riviera wanted to downsize the defense forces and open the doors to outsiders."

"Now you understand." Devon's tone was sympathetic and understanding. "His policies would mean the end of USC7 as we know it. This has been a functioning, thriving democracy for thirty years. If rigging an election or torturing those who want to take that from us means another thirty years of survival, I'm okay with that? Are you?"

Maya could not answer. She still tried to deal with everything she had heard. This was the second time in as many days her world had been shattered and turned upside down.

"Can't we let the survivors from USC5 in or send out people to help them get back on their feet?"

Devon shook his head. "We estimate there are ten to fifteen thousand people left alive in Albany. We could never handle such a strain on our resources. Besides, the guy in command of that facility runs it like his own private fiefdom. Most of those who survived are thugs like him." Devon pointed to the chairs behind him. "You saw what they're like."

Maya had. She had been horrified watching Devon interrogate them, but that couldn't compare to the terror of what would happen if these people took over.

"Maya, you have a good heart and your intentions are well placed, but we no longer have that luxury. If they attack us in force, we won't be able to defend ourselves. This is a battle for our survival. It's us or them. And the odds are stacked against us."

Devon pushed himself off the table, kissed Maya on the forehead, and left.

Maya dropped into the chair and stared at the two-way mirror. What had happened to her life? Seven weeks ago, she had been living in blissful ignorance like almost everyone else here. Now she knew the utopia she had grown up to admire was a farce, and her lover played a willing part. Even worse, a more horrible fate awaited them, and nothing they could do would stop it. As much as she hated knowing this, she could not turn her back on reality. She would have to live with everything she had witnessed and been involved with. More importantly, she needed to prepare for the upcoming battle. Knowing what she did, she couldn't stand by and watch these people take over her world.

Then her thoughts drifted to her family. Shit, what would

happen to them if these people invaded? It took several minutes to calm her fears and push the horrible images from her mind.

What had happened to her life?

You grew up, Maya chastised herself. You went from being a young woman to an adult overnight. Welcome to the real world. How do you plan on handling it?

Maya already knew the answer. It only took time to come to terms with it. Tomorrow she would track down Devon and tell him she was on board with everything. She would do whatever it took to preserve the integrity of USC7 and would deal with her conscience later. That is what her father and mother expected of her. That's what she expected of herself.

Maya headed back to the barracks with a determination she had never experienced before.

CHAPTER FIFTEEN

B RAD PETERSON DROVE his maintenance cart through the dank corridors of New Empire, the title given to USC5 twenty-four years ago by Caesar, the self-appointed ruler of the facility. Peterson remembered what this place looked like in the early days, though many of the memories had faded with age. He had entered the facility along with his parents and younger sister when six, a young boy excited by his new life underground and oblivious to the catastrophe taking place on the surface. He recalled the bright lights, the glistening floors and walls, and the sense of optimism among the citizens that they would make it through the Great Freeze and thrive.

That sense of optimism seemed as distant and faded as Peterson's memories.

The corridors were now dingy, scuff marks covering the walls and litter and ground-in dirt marring the once pristine floor. Damages to the interior went unrepaired. Over time, more than half the lighting had failed, with no one bothering to replace the bulbs. Crime worsened, with some sections becoming so bad even the IDF refused to enter them. Now despair and fear replaced the optimism that once thrived down here.

The trouble began their second year below ground. Computer malfunctions took offline one-third of their water processing plants, a situation worsened when half the hydroponic units broke down. With food supplies reduced by fifty percent, the first governor—Peterson could not recall his name—took the only action possible and put the citizens on half rations until the processing plants and hydroponic units were repaired. They never were. The problems stemmed from a software design flaw the programmers were unable to fix. The facility survived on half rations for nearly months until the design flaw took twenty percent of the remaining hydroponic units offline. The governor responded with more food rationing.

Unfortunately for the elites, news spread that they continued to receive full rations. While four-fifths of the facility starved, those in Ring B held dinner parties. A food riot broke out that was quickly and violently quelled by the defense forces, leaving over three thousand citizens dead or wounded. That led to a revolution by those in Rings C and D. When the rumors of ration hoarding by the elite turned out to be true, everyone from Ring B, as well as those citizens from other rings who supported the old system, were banished. Over twenty thousand people were cast out onto Above Earth to freeze to death. It only improved the situation temporarily. The triumvirate chosen by the revolutionaries had to maintain half rationing while promising to restore order.

They failed miserably. The design flaw in the computer imbedded itself in the system, and soon an additional thirty percent of the hydroponic units failed. Soon, livestock began to die off. The leadership's inability to fix the food situation became compounded when the citizens discovered that the triumvirate and their followers who took over Ring B had begun living like the elite they had banished. More riots broke out, each brutally put down by the defense forces. The triumvirate decided to rectify the situation by decreasing USC5's population by half. They started with political opponents, anyone who spoke negatively against the new government, and those deemed unworthy of survival, including older citizens. Daily public executions took place in the ceremonial hall. Peterson remembered watching the bodies being loaded onto carts and taken to the elevator bay to be disposed of topside. Their reign of terror lasted almost a year.

Then Antoni Caesar entered the picture. One of the computer programmers unable to correct the software error that brought down the hydroponic units, he had been slated along with his colleagues for execution. Caesar led a revolution against the triumvirate, this time with the full backing of the defense forces, which had lost many of its officers to the purge. When the dust settled, Caesar became the ruler of USC5, now renamed the New Empire. By then, the population had dwindled to seventy thousand.

Caesar considered himself to be another Julius Caesar, the Emperor who restored order and glory to Rome. He had been in the beginning. Now he reigned more like Caligula.

Peterson came to the wall that cut off New Syracuse from the rest of the facility. He turned left and headed along a corridor that had few lights.

With more than half the population dead, Caesar moved the remaining citizens into one half of the facility and closed four sectors—New Syracuse, New Manhattan, New Queens, and New Long Island. He cut power to those areas to conserve energy. Within two months, rats and cockroaches spawned in the vacant spaces. Caesar sent in teams to capture the vermin and butcher the rats, their meat added to what little the livestock provided. The roaches were ground up and added to the livestock's food, freeing up the remaining hydroponics for the citizens. Rumor had it that some of the ground roaches were added to the facility's protein bars, but Peterson hoped that was merely gossip. As gross as it sounded, the food additives had the desired effect. Within three months, Caesar had restored rations to three-quarters capacity. Within a year, livestock thrived again and enough hydroponic units were jury-rigged that the facility's food supplies were able to keep up with the demand.

Then things took an ugly turn.

Caesar used his popularity to establish complete dominance, making himself ruler for life. He chose as his leadership men and women with so much blood on their hands, and so many skeletons in their closet, that none of them would challenge his authority out of fear of Caesar revealing their dirty secrets. He brutally crushed any opposition, those who disagreed either being quietly executed or banished to Above Earth. The citizens were urged to report any negative talk against the system to the authorities. Those who grumbled discontent or committed so-called crimes against the state were severely punished. The men were placed on half rations and consigned to the sub-basement where the dirtiest chores were handled, effectively becoming a prison system. Women spent five years working in the brothel where mistreatment and murder were commonplace.

Living quarters and common areas deteriorated in quality. The vermin from the closed-off sections multiplied a thousand-fold and made their way into the rest of the facility. Crime ran rampant in Rings D and E, with gangs forming in each sector. They extorted food from the locals and created their own drugs and alcohol, which a growing number of citizens used to dull the misery of their existence. Caesar turned a blind eye to this, allowing the gangs to run their sectors so long as they handed over dissidents to him. Over the years, thousands died by being turned in, many of them innocent. And, of course, the gangs had to do Caesar's bidding. One gang in New Buffalo challenged his authority. They were strung up in Ring E and left to the mercy of the citizens they had terrorized. After that, the remaining gangs fell into line. His father once referred to the facility as a "fucking ghetto," although Peterson had no idea what he meant.

That was how he came to work for Caesar eleven years ago.

Someone had overheard his father's remark and turned him in. Caesar exiled his parents onto Above Earth. Peterson could either freeze to death or stay behind and swear an oath of allegiance to Caesar. He chose the latter to save his younger sister, Charlotte. Caesar rewarded Peterson by making him a member of the inner circle yet reminded him who was in charge by taking Charlotte as one of his concubines. As twisted as the situation was, at least she was alive.

Peterson eventually became Caesar's right-hand man. He repressed the memories of what he had to do to keep himself and his sister safe—the betrayals, the forced gang rape of female dissidents, and the murders committed. He kept those memories repressed by using his power to help citizens on those rare occasions that he could and through heavily drinking the rot-gut whiskey produced by the gangs. His doctor called him a functioning alcoholic. Peterson saw himself as a survivor.

One of only twenty-eight thousand left in New Empire.

Peterson turned left into New Buffalo at the end of the corridor, the section set up as the facility's brothel. The girls lived and performed their services in the quarters along this section of Ring E. It also served as home to the facility's black market, which resembled a Middle East bizarre. Tents and covered tables lined the outer wall. Here one could buy medicines, drugs, cheap liquor, or any other commodity not readily available. One tent carried a sign saying the proprietor could arrange any sexual perversion imaginable—for a price.

Jacob, who ran Ring E, spotted Peterson approaching. He concluded his business with one of the gang members, slid a pouch of meth into his pocket, and flagged him down.

"What's up, Jake?"

"I wanted to give you this." Jacob reached into his back pocket and removed a dented metal flask. "I thought you'd want this. It's some of the good stuff. Not that swill they usually make."

"Thanks." Accepting the bribe, Peterson laid the flask on the seat beside him. "How are you doing?"

"Not good. Three girls committed suicide this week. The others are picking up the slack. Any chance I can get replacements?"

Fuck. Now he would have to find three more girls to endure this nightmare. "I'll see what I can do."

"Thanks. It's quiet now. Do you want one of the girls to give you a freebie?"

"No, thanks. I'm—"

Thankfully, the squawking over his radio saved him from an unpleasant situation.

"Sorry, I got to go." Peterson pulled away and, when out of earshot, keyed his radio. "What's up?"

"It's Mike down in coms. We haven't heard from Rat Trap in two days."

"Is it possible their radio is down?"

"It's possible, but it worked fine last time they checked in."

"Have you tried other frequencies?"

"We tried every frequency we agreed upon but got nothing." A pause. "Do you want me to inform Caesar?"

"I'm heading there now. I'll tell him. Let me know if there's any change."

"I will. And thanks."

Peterson knew Mike meant it. No one liked bringing the Boss bad news.

Continuing until the end of New Buffalo, Peterson turned left again and headed for Ring B. Caesar rarely used the governor's office anymore to conduct business, ostensibly because such a confined space was beneath him. Peterson assumed Caesar didn't want to remind the citizens of how much freedom they used to have under the original government. Large meetings were held in the ceremonial room where the executions occurred, a reminder to those attending what their fate would be if they challenged him. Personal meetings were conducted in Caesar's private quarters. God only knew what Peterson would find when he arrived. He once briefed Caesar on conditions in New Empire during an orgy.

Upon entering Ring B of New Buffalo, he stopped at the

first of three security checkpoints set up at either end of the corridor, each heavily armed. The guards frisked Peterson and checked the cart. If any weapons snuck through, the guard who allowed it through would be banished to Above Earth, or worse. The next two checkpoints were more perfunctory. Peterson parked a hundred feet from Caesar's private quarters. Four guards outside the residence waved him through. He knocked.

"Just a minute," came Caesar's voice from the other side. A few seconds later, he yelled, "Come in."

Peterson entered.

Caesar zipped up a pair of leather pants. The two women with him were straightening their dresses. Charlotte smiled at her brother and discreetly waved, then sat by the window and stared out at the blank screen. The video displays had not worked in decades. The other woman, a tall redhead he did not recognize but Caesar called Maxine, disappeared into the bathroom.

Caesar had let himself go over the past few years. A paunch formed around his waist and drooped over the top of his pants. His chest and arms had lost their muscular tone. His dark hair had grown long and unkempt, not having been washed in days. However, no one dared mess with him. Caesar still had enough strength to take on anyone in the facility and win. Anyone who doubted that need only study his green eyes that portrayed the brutality that lurked within the man.

"You're early."

"Sorry. I just received news from comms that Rat Trap's team hasn't checked in the last two days. I thought you'd want to know."

"Any idea what happened to them?" Caesar motioned to a set of chairs in the corner and slid into one.

"No idea." Peterson took the other chair. "It could be a problem with their radio. They gave no indication of having been spotted by USC7 personnel."

"It could be polar bears. They've been a nuisance lately. We might not consider feeding them so much." Caesar laughed. "When do their replacements arrive?"

"They should be there in a few hours. We'll know more then." Peterson chose his next words carefully. "If they were discovered, how will this affect our plans?"

"It won't change them one bit." Caesar leaned forward in his chair, his voice tinged with a menacing tone. "I trust everything is ready for the attack."

"Yes, sir. We've scrounged up all the cold-weather gear we could find and even ransacked the closed sections for boots and warm clothing. All the weapons have been serviced and we have enough ammunition to complete the job. Anything that we could use as a weapon has been rounded up. The machine shops have produced swords and knives for every member of the expedition. We'll be set to go in two days as planned."

"Excellent. You did well. I knew I could rely on you."

Though meant as a compliment, the words cut deep into what remained of Peterson's soul. "You do realize we're going to lose a lot of people on this march?"

"Irrelevant." Caesar brushed away the comment with a wave of his hand. "Only the weak will die. They deserve no better. The strong will survive. Once we take USC7, those who live will rightfully bask in the glory that is New Empire."

Peterson remained stoic. He dealt with a madman. If only he had the courage to kill Caesar and prevent this nightmare from happening. Sadly, he did not. Now he would oversee the destruction of another facility and the slaughter it entailed.

CHAPTER SIXTEEN

MAYA DID NOT return to the barracks until shortly before lights out. Carver and Medugno were out on patrol. Those who had gone topside chatted excitedly about Above Earth to the ones yet to go. It took a few minutes before she noticed bunk seven was empty.

"What happened to Barbie?"

Bettany moved close and lowered her voice. "She packed up her personal belongings and left about an hour ago."

"What happened?"

"Her Carbine jammed during weapons training. She turned toward Byrd to ask for help, accidentally aiming the barrel at him while still pulling the trigger. Byrd ripped the weapon out of her hand, slapped her across the face, and screamed at her for being an ass, telling her that's how you get someone killed. The poor girl couldn't take it. She broke down, cried, and ran away."

"What's going to happen to her?"

Bettany shrugged. "She's definitely out of the defense forces. My guess is there'll be repercussions for her leaving like that. Probably charges of abandoning her post or dereliction of duty, something to make an example out of her so others stay in line. I feel bad for Barbie, but it's for the best. She didn't fit in here."

Byrd entered. "Well, I see the force's favorite cadet has finally returned. Fall in."

Maya braced herself. She stood at attention with the others.

Byrd paced the aisle. "Okay, people. Today we've seen the worst and the best our cadets have to offer. Barbie fucked up big time and is no longer a part of our glorious training program. I hope the rest of you sewer roaches learned a valuable lesson. And we have a trained killer among our group."

He stopped in front of Maya. She prepared for the worst.

"Cadet Santos saved Lieutenant Haskell's life today by killing a polar bear while on patrol." He turned to Maya. "Congratulations, cadet."

"Thank you, sir."

"It's good to know someone here listens to me. Because of Cadet Santos, I'm extending lights out by thirty minutes tonight. I suggest you use that time to find out how she did it. That's a skill you're all going to need soon enough."

Byrd gave an approving nod to Maya and exited.

Once the drill instructor left, the others gathered around Maya, honestly anxious to hear what happened. Maya told them the details, excluding the fact that the polar bear was a human. She told them how she felt while doing it and stressed the importance of their training.

Maya didn't know if Byrd knew the truth or had been fed a lie by the higher-ups. She knew one thing for certain, though.

Before too long, each of her fellow cadets would have to take a life, or more, to survive.

CHAPTER SEVENTEEN

EVON STOOD BY the end of the prisoner's hospital bed, studying the man. The guards had strapped the prisoner to the bed by his ankles and wrists, with two more straps around his chest and another securing his upper legs. The bastard would not be able to move. All part of the plan.

He glanced over at Maria.

"Bring him around."

"Are you sure? He'll be in a lot of pain."

"That's the plan." Devon made eye contact with Maria and motioned to the IV inserted into the prisoner's arm.

Taking a syringe from off the nearby tray, Maria injected Ritalin into the vent. Jimmy moaned and moved his head. His eyes slowly opened.

"Where am I?" Jimmy asked groggily.

"Leave us alone, please," Devon said to Maria. She nodded and exited the room.

"Where am I?" Panic started to set in as Jimmy realized he could not move.

"Relax. You're in the med bay."

"Why am I strapped down?"

"To prevent you from moving, of course."

Jimmy yanked on the restraints and winced.

"You're strapped in tight. There's no way you're getting out. Besides, the more you struggle, the greater the pain."

Jimmy continued pulling against the restraints. He grimaced and went limp.

"Why does my abdomen hurt?"

"You mean this?" Devon placed his forefinger on a row of stitches that ran across a bulge in Jimmy's abdomen and pushed.

"Fuck!"

"We killed a sewer rat, opened you up, and wrapped your intestines around it. The pain you're feeling is it starting to rot. The decay will soon spread to your intestines and slowly make its way through your body. This is nothing compared to what you'll experience in three days."

"Are you out of your fucking mind?" screamed Jimmy.

Devon made a gesture of massaging his ear. "Scream all you want. In a couple of days, you won't have the energy to talk."

Jimmy broke down and cried. "Why are you doing this to me?"

Devon laughed. "You can't figure it out?"

The prisoner shook his head.

Devon stepped closer and leaned over to whisper. "I gave you a chance to cooperate, but you refused. Now we're playing it my way." Devon ran his fingers along the IV tubing. "I've ordered the nurses to administer a regimen of antibiotics. Not enough to cure the infection, just prolong it and add to your agony. Oh, and you won't be receiving any morphine. I figure you'll be dead in a week. In three days, you'll be wishing it would happen sooner."

"Please don't do this to me."

"You're doing this to yourself. Once you tell me everything I want to know, we'll remove the rat and nurse you back to health. In the meantime…." Devon pulled over the stand with the monitoring equipment and positioned it so it faced Jimmy. "You can watch your vital signs to see how rapidly your body is deteriorating. Tell the nurse when you're ready to talk."

Devon gave Jimmy's foot a friendly pat and headed for the door, pausing before he left. "By the way, remember the three soldiers you ambushed the other day and murdered?"

"Yeah?"

"One of them was the nurse's husband, so don't expect any sympathy from her. Talk to you soon."

Once in the corridor, Devon caught Maria's attention. "You have it from here."

"Do you want me to keep you advised on his condition?"

"No. Call me only when he's ready to talk."

"Yes, sir."

Devon left med bay. He had to prepare for a meeting with the Governor in an hour.

CHAPTER EIGHTEEN

M ANGERIAN SAT IN a winged-back chair placed in front of her desk. She leaned into one corner, exhausted, trying her best to stay awake. This past week had been overwhelming between the elections and finding the three operatives from USC5 recording their guard schedule. She had hoped to avoid both encounters. Fate decided otherwise. Now she had to deal with them simultaneously. To cope, the governor had been swigging two pots of the strongest coffee the facility had to offer each day, pretty much black sludge. No one knew that, for the past two days, she had also been taking Adderall as a stimulant and would continue to do so as long as it didn't cloud her judgment.

The governor started with Devon. "What did you learn from the prisoners?"

"Nothing yet."

"You said you could get them to talk."

"And I will, but not right away. Sometimes you have to wear down the will a little."

"You murdered one of them," growled Donahue, the Administrator of the Interior.

"Correction," said Arasaki. "I executed him for murdering three EDF personnel."

"With a baseball bat? Is it true you're torturing the remaining prisoner to get him to talk?"

Devon remained stoic. "We're using enhanced interrogation techniques."

"In other words, you're torturing him."

"Dammit, Jeff. You know what they did to our people. He got what he deserved. We're not talking about police brutality but an overt act of aggression against us. We're about to go to war with USC5." Mangerian met Devon's gaze. "Or am I exaggerating?"

"I'm afraid not, ma'am. Based on the intelligence we found on the prisoners, I assess with ninety-five percent certainty that USC5 is planning an attack on our facility."

"Do you concur, General Arasaki?"

The general nodded.

"Do we know when the attack will take place?" asked Mangerian.

"No, ma'am," said Devon. "I'll hopefully get all the intelligence we need about the attack once the prisoner talks."

The Governor thought for a moment. "General Arasaki, how prepared are we for an attack?"

"We're at peak performance, ma'am. Our weapons and equipment are in excellent shape, and we have more than enough ammunition to ward off an attack. If need be, we still have plenty of defense force personnel to add to our ranks. Fortunately for us, the only way into the facility is through the upper bay. In a worst-case scenario, all we need to do is close the bay doors and lock the elevator in place. The cold will take care of them."

"What if they have explosives and breach the bay doors?" asked Mangerian.

Arasaki skipped over the flaw in his plan. "I doubt it'll be an issue. USC5 was assigned the same number of weapons as USC7. The battle line-up is even, two thousand troops each. We also have the advantage of being on the defensive."

"And what if they have more than two thousand men?" asked Thompson, Chief of Security.

"We don't know that," Arasaki responded angrily.

"Hang on," snapped Mangerian. "What are you not telling me?"

Devon jumped in. "It's a probability that USC5 has weapons other than those issued before the Great Freeze."

"You don't believe that?" asked Arasaki.

"We found the three snowmobiles used by the prisoners. They were jury-rigged with parts from a Hagglund. If they can do that with their vehicles, the chances are excellent they've done the same with weapons. It's also a possibility they could use a swarm attack against us."

Mangerian creased her eyebrows. "What do you mean by swarm attack?"

"The Red Army used the tactic in World War II. They would send penal battalions and untrained troops against enemy defenses to clear minefields and use up the enemy's ammo. Then the best troops would move in and overwhelm their defenses."

The Governor sighed. "How many are we talking about?"

"It's hard to say, ma'am."

"Give me your best estimate."

"We estimate there are between ten and fifteen thousand citizens alive in USC5. Assuming they take all abled-bodied males with them, we could be looking at an attack force of five to eight thousand."

Arasaki leaned back on the sofa and brushed Devon aside with a wave of his hand. "You pulled that number out of your ass."

"On the contrary, it's the most accurate estimate based on the intelligence we have."

"Explain," ordered Thompson.

"The last communication we received from USC5 reported that half their hydroponic units and one-third of their water processing plants had broken down. My analysts calculated these figures based on the number of humans who could be sustained with those productivity levels. I admit it's only an estimate. Depending on what happened over the last twenty-eight years, that number could be higher or lower."

"Fucking great." Mangerian rubbed her eyes.

"The plan remains the same either way," advised Arasaki. "We kill as many as possible during the attack and then close down the facility and leave the rest to freeze to death."

"And what if they breach the bay? Are we capable of defending ourselves?"

Arasaki lowered his head.

"Thompson?"

"If we go with Devon's estimate, it's doubtful we could defend the facility."

Donahue glanced at the others. "Are you implying they could overrun us?"

"I'm stating it as a fact," said Thompson. "It's unlikely we could hold out against more than three thousand people."

Denning, who had remained silent the entire meeting, leaned forward on the sofa. "We do have another defensive strategy, but it's extreme."

"No!" blurted Arasaki. "I refuse to——."

Mangerian held up her hand, cutting off the general. Her gaze narrowed on Denning. "Go on."

The colonel spent the next five minutes laying out the details of his proposal. Everyone stared at him, stunned, except for Devon, who nodded his approval. When Denning finished, he sat back and waited for a decision.

Mangerian pondered the plan. "You realize the implications of what you're suggesting?"

"I do, ma'am."

"Madame Governor," began Devon. "You realize the implications of USC5 taking over our facility?"

Mangerian cast him a withering glance that quickly devolved into determination. "I do."

"Is there anyone else who disagrees with this plan?"

Donahue and Thompson averted their gaze.

"Gentlemen, I want an answer. I'm not making this decision without input from you."

"No," offered Thompson. "It's the only way to defend ourselves."

"It's barbaric," mumbled Donahue.

"What was that?"

"It's barbaric." The Chief of the Interior met the Governor's gaze. "Isn't there any other way?"

Mangerian spoke with a calm, consoling tone. "If you can think of anything better, now's the time to offer it."

Donahue remained silent.

"We'll keep the plan as a last-ditch solution. I'm not ruling it out yet, but it's too early to go with that option. Is everyone in agreement?"

Everyone responded in the affirmative. Mangerian dismissed them. When the last person left, she returned to her desk and buzzed her secretary that she did not want to be disturbed.

Mangerian agreed with Donahue. What she considered was barbaric. She would only use it as a last resort. But what other choice did she have? The safety of USC7, of the two hundred thousand citizens she had sworn to protect, rested on her shoulders. She could refuse to initiate it and pray that the facility did not fall, or she could go ahead and be responsible for mass slaughter. Either way, she would have to live with this on her conscience for the rest of her life.

A part of her wished Riviera had won the election.

CHAPTER NINETEEN

B EAST LOOKED AT his map and swore to himself. Their bearings had been five miles off and they missed the rendezvous point with Rat Trap's team. They had passed by USC7 without realizing it, discovering their error only when they reached the outskirts of Boston. Recalculating their position, they backtracked, arriving at the facility four hours behind schedule. It took another two and a half hours to find the ice cave Rat Trap had commandeered.

Pulling their snowmobiles next to the entrance, Beast and his team dismounted.

Cody pointed to the entrance as he unslung his Carbine and raised it into the low-ready position.

"Looks like they ran into trouble."

Cody referred to the splotch of frozen blood in the snow and the bullet holes carved into the ice.

"No shit, asshole. I can see good enough."

Cody flipped him the finger.

"Do you think it was polar bears?" asked Kevin.

"Since when do fucking polar bears carry M4s?" spat Beast. "Go check it out."

"Why me?"

"Because you're the one asking stupid questions. Now move."

Kevin inched his way to the entrance and peered inside. He turned to Beast, who motioned for him to enter. Kevin obeyed. A moment later, he stuck his head through the entrance and waved for the others to join him.

The interior was barren. Everything belonging to Rat Trap's team, even personal items, had been removed. The residue of tear gas still emanated from the walls.

"Do you think they were discovered and abandoned their position?" asked Cody.

Beast shook his head. "We gotta assume they were captured."

"Do you think they talked?" Panic grew inside Kevin. "If they did, they'll know what we're planning."

"Rat Trap won't talk, and neither will the others."

"Are you sure about that?"

"Shut up and quit being a pussy."

"Do we stay here?" asked Cody.

"Just for tonight. In the morning, we'll find another place to stay in case—"

Kevin held up his hand, cutting off Beast.

"What the hell is wrong with you?"

"Listen."

The three men heard a vehicle approaching.

RAMON MANEUVERED THE Hagglund toward the snow cave where the other EDF team had uncovered the spies from USC5 a few days ago. He had a few extra minutes before he needed to return to the facility and, since he was within two miles of the location, decided to swing by and check it out.

As he made his way up a shallow snowdrift, sudden movement to the left attracted his attention, accompanied by Mikos shouting.

"God damn!"

"What is it?" asked Ramon.

"It's only a polar bear," chuckled So-young from the rear. "You almost ran over him while he slept."

Ramon looked out the side window. A polar bear weighing

close to five hundred pounds scampered across the ice, its head turned to stare at the passing vehicle. If looks could kill, they would all be dead. Ramon didn't care. It wasn't the glare that worried him but those giant paws.

Topping the drift, the snow cave sat three hundred yards away.

So-young leaned forward between the seats. "Didn't one of the previous teams retrieve the snowmobiles they found out here?"

"Yeah. So?"

"What are those three doing outside the cave?"

Ramon mumbled a curse under his breath. He had Mikos report their finding to USC7 as he steered the Hagglund to the right and approached the cave from the flank, stopping it by the snowmobiles.

"What did headquarters say?"

"They told us to wait until reinforcements arrived."

"How long?"

Mikos shrugged. "At least an hour."

"Screw that," Ramon replied.

"Headquarters told us to wait."

"Whoever's in that cave will figure out by then that we're here. I want to move now while we still have the advantage. Let's go. Try and take them alive, if possible."

The three EDF soldiers climbed out and, Carbines at the ready, made their way to the cave.

Three men rushed out of the cave, spun around, and fired into the opening.

Ramon raised his Carbine into the high-ready position. "Drop your weapons!"

The three men replaced their magazines and continued firing, either ignoring or not hearing Ramon's order.

Ramon's team inched closer. "I said, drop your weapons!"

One of the intruders, a beast of a man, glanced over at Ramon. "Help us out, man. We ran into a den of polar bears."

Ramon moved to within ten feet of them. "This is your last chance! Drop your weapons or—"

The three intruders swung their Carbines on Ramon's team. Two fired, killing Ramon instantly and hitting Mikos in the left shoulder. Mikos dropped his weapon and fell onto the ice, his right hand clutching the wound.

So-young hesitated, caught off guard by the sudden takedown of her friends.

Beast trained his Carbine on So-young. "Drop your weapon if you want to live."

So-young cursed Ramon for being so stupid. He had allowed these assholes to get the drop on them. Knowing she could not win a firefight against three gunmen, she bent over and placed her Carbine on the ice.

BEAST GRINNED. IF taking out the rest of the USC7 defense forces proved as easy as overpowering these three, capturing the facility would be a cinch.

Cody and Kevin stepped up to Ramon and Mikos. Kevin slammed the butt of his weapon into Mikos' face. Mikos stirred and moaned. Kevin hit him again, knocking out the man.

Beast walked up to So-young. He pulled down the hood of her parka and ripped off her beanie. Her long brunette hair spilled down her back.

"Well, well. What do we have here?"

So-young remained silent.

Beast slapped her across the face, the blow softened by his heavy gloves.

"You can make this easy or difficult. I don't care."

"I'm Corporal Kim So-young of the EDF."

"I assume you know what happened to our friends."

"One was killed when he attacked our people. The other two are prisoners."

"Which means they're being tortured for information."

"We're not animals like you."

Beast punched So-young in the face, the blow cushioned by his gloves but powerful enough to knock her off balance. She kicked Beast in the groin with the heel of her boot, which would have taken him down if his gear had not contained so much padding. Grabbing So-young by the collar, Beast dragged her to him and head-butted her. She dropped to her knees, dazed.

He evaluated the situation. He motioned to Cody and Kevin and pointed to the unconscious EDF soldiers.

"Strip those two of their clothes and weapons. Load their gear in the Hagglund. It's ours now."

"What should we do with them?"

"Leave them to freeze."

Cody nodded.

"Then get me a pair of pliers from the snowmobiles." Beast stood so he towered over So-young. "I'm going to show this bitch how we treat our prisoners."

CHAPTER TWENTY

AGONY WRACKED JIMMY'S body. The decay from the dead rat had spread to his intestines. The pain was unbearable. Chills raced through his body and sweat poured down his clammy forehead. He had already soiled himself three times today with bloody diarrhea. No one had changed his bedding, so he lay in his own filth, the rancid mess covering his buttocks, upper legs, and testicles. Although he could not see the mess, he smelled it. The odor stank of feces and rotting flesh. It filled the room and permeated his nostrils, churning the contents of his stomach into a sickening mess.

"Nurse!"

No one responded.

Jimmy took a deep breath and screamed.

"Nuurrssee!"

The minimal effort upset his already weakened body. Pain shot through his abdomen as if someone had twisted his intestines. Jimmy felt a fourth round of diarrhea flow from his body. His anus burned. His stomach roiled and heaved. Leaning his head to one side, Jimmy puked, spreading the vomitus across his pillow. Chunks rested on his shoulder and dripped from his lips. He spit several times, trying to clear his mouth of the foul taste.

Leaning his head back against the pillow, Jimmy cried.

A few minutes later, Maria entered the room wearing a mask, a rubber apron, and latex gloves.

"What's going on in here? I can smell it at the nurses' station."

"Can someone... clean me up?"

Maria walked over to the bed and feigned concern. "That is pretty disgusting. I'll have the night shift change you."

"Please... do it now."

Maria shook her head. "No."

"I'm... burning up. I think... I have a fever."

Removing a hand-held thermometer from her pocket, she ran it across Jimmy's forehead.

"Do I... have a fever?"

"Oh, yeah. It's a hundred and two point five. Looks like you have sepsis."

"Wh... what's that?"

"It means your intestines have ruptured and fecal matter is spreading through your body. The infection and pain are going to get a lot worse. Don't worry, though. You'll be dead in a few days."

"Help me. Please."

"Sorry." Maria smiled beneath her mask. "I'm under orders not to do anything for you. Come to think of it, I might get in trouble if I have your sheets changed."

Maria turned to leave.

"Wait," blurted Jimmy.

"Is there anything else?"

"Yes. Tell Major Williams I'm ready to talk."

CHAPTER TWENTY-ONE

MAYA WAS GLAD to be able to concentrate on basic training after recent events. It distracted her from thinking about the nightmare the facility would soon face. Being with her fellow cadets made her feel comfortable. They had bonded over the past seven weeks, even Sanchez. She had heard Devon mention once the "leave no one behind" mentality. At the time, she did not understand the sentiment, though now it became clear. Your fellow soldiers become close like a family or, more appropriately, a brotherhood. Maya knew every member of the unit would do anything possible to keep each other safe. That trust and camaraderie are what kept the defense forces strong.

More importantly, though, Maya needed the training. Soon she would be facing the enemy in combat and wanted to be as prepared as possible.

Byrd entered the gym and motioned for the seven cadets to gather around him. "I only have a week left to turn you sewer roaches into something resembling a fighting unit. Today we're switching from weapons training to something that will save your lives one day—hand-to-hand combat."

Maya winced. She dreaded this part of the training. She had never been confrontational, always avoiding fights in high school. Shooting at an enemy from a distance was one thing, but getting in close and having physical contact scared her. Maya told herself to suck it up.

"Today, you're going to learn Krav Maga, a military hand-to-hand combat technique developed by the Israel Defense

Forces. Krav Maga is derived from a combination of techniques such as boxing, wrestling, judo, Akido, and karate but with an emphasis on street-fighting. The idea of Krav Maga is to take the most effective and practical techniques of other fighting styles and make them teachable to military conscripts. Krav Maga emphasizes aggression as well as simultaneous defensive and offensive maneuvers. The difference between Krav Maga and traditional fighting methods is that it teaches you to fight to survive, not to fight fairly. You'll learn to continue to strike your opponent until they're dead or incapacitated using any object you can. You sewer roaches will learn to attack an opponent and target the body's most vulnerable points, such as the eyes, neck, throat, face, solar plexus, groin, ribs, knees, feet, finger, and liver. By the time you've completed your training, these moves will become second nature to you."

Maya wanted to add that the cadets will need them soon enough but thought better of it.

"Carver, get over here."

The cadet joined Byrd.

"The easiest way for an opponent to take you down is to get you in a rear chokehold. The opponent uses his choking arm to apply pressure to the trachea and cut off your oxygen. In five seconds, your opponent will have you on the floor and unconscious. Carver, put me in a chokehold but don't apply pressure."

Byrd turned his back to Carver. The cadet placed his left forearm across the instructor's throat, wrapped his right hand around his left wrist for leverage, and closed the hold.

"The natural reaction is to lean back into the hold. That only gives the advantage to your opponent and will get you killed. Instead, grab the opponent's arm and bend at your waist. That puts him off balance."

Byrd performed the maneuver until Carver stretched across his back.

"Then use your left hand to punch him in the groin followed by a gouge to the eyes."

Byrd simulated a punch to Carver's testicles with his left hand, then brought the same hand up, palm and fingers flat, and jabbed it over his shoulder toward Carver's eyes, stopping before making contact. The cadet involuntarily arched back. Byrd grabbed the cadet's right arm on his wrist and forearm, breaking the hold as he spun his body one-hundred-and eighty degrees. While still grasping Carver's wrist in his left hand, Byrd slid his right until it rested on Carver's upper arm. Carver remained off balance.

"By extra-rotating the opponent's arm, I can bring him down."

Byrd used his left hand to push Carver's right arm back. The cadet toppled over onto the floor.

"From this position, take out your opponent any way you can."

Byrd lifted Carver off the floor and patted him on the back. "Remember, the most important thing is to break that chokehold quickly. If your opponent is protecting their groin and eyes, use whatever means necessary to disorient them enough to loosen their grip within five seconds or you're dead. Let me show you again."

The drill instructor repeated the procedure on Carver five times, then switched out and let Carver defend himself. It seemed easy when the cadet performed it. After the last demonstration, Byrd stood.

"Break off into pairs and practice. Carver, you team up with Porky and Butterfingers."

Bettany moved over to Maya. "You're with me. I'll attack first."

She felt anxious when Bettany's arms wrapped around her neck and tightened. Maya froze.

"Come on," urged Bettany. "Remember the moves Byrd taught us."

Maya bent forward. Bettany's arm pressed against her

trachea.

"You have to grab my arm first."

Maya tried it again, this time clutching Bettany's arm. As she bent, she slid her hand between her friend's thighs, simulating a punch, then repeated the move toward her eyes. It took her three attempts to execute the reverse turn properly. Once she got that down, Maya found it easy to twist Bettany to the ground. The maneuver had not been as difficult as she thought. But then, she was sparring with a friend and not engaged in a life-or-death battle with an enemy.

After thirty minutes of practice, Byrd called the cadets back together and walked through another defensive move, followed by thirty minutes of practice. They kept up this routine all morning and well into the afternoon. By the time Byrd ordered them back to the barracks, each cadet was exhausted and had suffered numerous bruises.

Yet they were much more confident than eight hours earlier.

CHAPTER TWENTY-TWO

WHEN DEVON ARRIVED at the autopsy lab, Governor Mangerian, General Arasaki, and Colonel Denning waited in the corridor.

"What's going on?" asked Mangerian.

"One of our patrols went missing last night. They were found dead this morning by the snow cave where we captured the prisoners the other day. Whoever did it took the Hagglund and all their gear."

"And you think it's another recon party?"

"I know it is." Devon did not attempt to hide the concern in his eyes. "The team leader brought the bodies back. She said they were in bad shape. I wanted you to see for yourselves."

The door to the autopsy room opened, allowing a wave of chilled air to wash into the corridor. An older woman, probably in her mid-fifties, centered herself in the doorway. She wore a thick surgical gown, two pairs of latex gloves, and a surgical face shield.

"Sorry, Madame Governor. I didn't realize you were here already until I heard you talking. I'm Dr. Stigliano." She removed the glove from her right hand and greeted her visitors. "Please, come in."

As they entered, Governor Mangerian asked, "Is the autopsy complete?"

"No need to do." Stigliano threw the gloves into a yellow metal bin adorned with a Biohazard warning label, then tossed in the face shield. She moved toward the autopsy table and two stretchers in the middle of the room. "The causes of death were obvious."

The twin stretchers contained the naked bodies of Mikos and Ramone. Plastic zip ties bound the ankles and wrists together. Both were curled into a fetal position, expressions of agony etched onto their faces.

"These two were stripped naked and left to freeze. There are indications of bruising on their faces and heads, and one has a fractured skull, presumably from being knocked unconscious by the butt of an M4. They were the lucky ones."

Stigliano slid off her operating gown, rolled it into a ball, and placed it on one of the stretchers. She headed for the autopsy table where So-young's body lay prone. Stigliano pulled back the sheet covering the body. The Governor gasped.

So-young had been brutalized. Her vagina and anus showed signs of abuse with severe injuries and traces of blood. Bruises extended from her shoulders down to her wrists, where she had been held down while being raped repeatedly. Her face contained multiple contusions, including a broken nose and a swollen right eye. Heavy bruising covered her nipples and areola. Yet none of this compared to the incision that ran down her chest from her abdomen to her navel, exposing her internal organs.

Mangerian swallowed the bile rising in the back of her throat.

"This woman had been sexually assaulted numerous times and then tortured. The bruising on the breasts suggests someone used a pair of pliers on them. They also used the pliers to do this."

Stigliano pulled back So-young's lips, revealing swollen gums with tears in the skin and no teeth.

"Her assailants pulled out her teeth. They also made the incision along her chest to expose her internal organs and left her to die of exposure. With luck, she died quickly."

Mangerian averted her eyes and turned around, facing the wall. Stigliano recovered So-young's corpse with the sheet.

A tense silence filled the room. The Governor turned around, fury and determination in her eyes. She turned to Denning. "How long will it take to implement your plan?"

"Everything is ready to go. I can have the defenses set up within forty-eight hours. But we need to keep this secret from any spies in the area. If they get wind of this, it won't work."

"Understand. General Arasaki, increase the patrols around the bay area."

"I cannot be a part of this. If you proceed with the captain's plan, I'll have to resign my commission."

The Governor's teeth ground together. "So be it. Colonel Denning, you are now Acting Chief of the Defense Forces. Make all the necessary preparations and increase patrols around the bay. If you find anyone, try and take them alive for questioning."

"Yes, Madam Governor."

"One more thing," ordered Mangerian. "Not a word of this to anyone outside this room. I don't want to create a panic. We'll have a hard enough time stopping the enemy and don't need to waste our people quieting unrest among the citizens. Is that understood?"

Everyone responded in the affirmative. Mangerian left.

A dejected Arasaki walked over to Denning. "You know how I feel about this plan."

Denning nodded and motioned toward So-young. "It's the only way to stop this from happening to everyone here."

"I know. I just can't be a part of it. Good luck."

The general departed, followed by Denning.

Devon's radio crackled. "Lieutenant Williams, are you there?"

He keyed the talk button. "I'm here. What's up?"

"This is Maria. The prisoner wants to talk."

CHAPTER TWENTY-THREE

D EVON HAD CALLED Maya from the barracks to take part in the interrogation of the prisoner. Maya thought witnessing what Devon did to Rat Trap had been the worst thing she had endured until she stepped into Jimmy's room. Seeing him lashed to his hospital bed lying in his filth and smelling the ghastly odor made her want to puke. What kind of nightmares went on behind the scenes in the facility?

Devon motioned for her to stand at the head of Jimmy's bed while he stood at the end. Maria hovered in the corner of the room.

"Maria says you're ready to talk."

Jimmy nodded, even that minor motion producing pain.

"Nurse, please give him some morphine."

Maria stepped forward, filled a syringe with twenty-five milligrams of morphine, and injected it into the vent. Jimmy leaned his head back and relaxed.

"Thank you. Can I get some more?"

"If you cooperate. Now, what were you sent here to do?"

"Spy on you." Jimmy opened his eyes but did not sit up. "Our orders were to record your movements and make a schedule of your patrols so we know when USC7 is most vulnerable."

"Why?"

"Because Caesar is planning to attack this facility."

"Who's Caesar?"

"He's in charge of New Empire, or what you refer to as USC5."

Jimmy spent the next half hour filling them in on the history of the other facility, confirming some of what they knew, correcting several inaccurate assessments, and providing a wealth of new intelligence. Devon listened intently, expressing no emotion. Maya watched Jimmy for any signs of deception but detected none. He talked freely and answered all of Devon's questions without hesitation. By the time Jimmy finished, he needed to pause and catch his breath. Devon gave him a few seconds to relax.

"Are there any other teams watching us?"

Jimmy shook his head. "Just the one, though we rotate every month. There were two teams before us. Our replacements should be in place by now. They're the last."

"Why is that?"

"Because Caesar plans to attack you within a week."

"When and how?"

A glimmer of fear sparkled in Jimmy's eyes. He did not answer.

"Jimmy, when and how does Caesar plan to attack us?"

Silence.

Devon leaned forward, placed his palm on Jimmy's incisions, and pressed. Puss flowed between the stitches. The young man screamed. His bowels evacuated another round of bloody diarrhea, this time gushing toward the end of the bed. The nauseating stench proved too much for Maya to bear. She leaned behind the bed and vomited onto the floor. When she stood upright, Devon wiped his hands on a clean portion of the bedsheet.

"I'll ask one more time. When and how will Caesar attack?"

When Jimmy refused to answer, Devon placed his palm on the incisions, pushing longer and harder. Three of the stitches ruptured, shooting a stream of puss across the bed. A portion of rotting intestine extended through the opening. Jimmy screamed and thrashed around. For a moment, Maya thought he might black out. Devon continued applying pressure.

"Stop it! Stop it! I'll talk!"

Devon released his grip. "Go on."

Jimmy struggled to regain his composure. "The attack... is planned... for the twenty-eighth."

Maya's eyes widened. That was in eight days.

"How?"

"They're going to storm... the front gate during shift change." Jimmy gasped. "Once they have the bay... the facility is open to attack."

"We'll just keep the bay closed."

"They have explosives."

"That's insane. That would expose the whole facility to the weather."

"Caesar... is insane."

Devon thought for a moment. "Doesn't he realize it won't work? We're evenly matched when it comes to firearms, plus we have the advantage of the defense."

Jimmy breathed deep. "He's been producing bladed weapons... for a year. They now have... five times the weapons you do. He plans on using... a swarm attack... to overwhelm your defenses."

"Who'll be attacking?"

"The entire facility."

"How many people is that?"

"Twenty...." Jimmy's last word trailed off as pain overcame him.

"How many?"

"Twenty-eight thousand."

For the first time since Maya had known him, Devon seemed caught off guard.

"Did you say twenty-eight thousand?"

Jimmy nodded.

"*Thousand?*"

"Yes." Jimmy closed his eyes and rested.

Devon glanced over at Maya, fear glistening in his eyes. They both realized the defense forces could never defend the facility against such a number.

As Devon moved away from the bed, Jimmy opened his eyes. "Don't leave me like this."

Devon walked over to Maria. "Do you have more morphine?"

She pulled from her pocket a second syringe and a bottle of the pain killer. Devon filled the syringe with two hundred milligrams of morphine. Going back to the bed, Devon stuck the needle into the vent. Jimmy locked eyes with him. Instead of protesting, he nodded at Devon and smiled. Devon pressed the plunger, releasing the lethal amount of morphine into the IV.

A few seconds later, an expression of contentment washed over Jimmy's face. Maria waited a few minutes then checked Jimmy's pulse. He had passed on.

"What should I do with the body, sir?"

"Have it incinerated along with the mattress and sheets."

"Yes, sir." Maria escorted the two into the corridor. "Did I hear him right? Are we about to be attacked by an army of twenty-eight thousand people?"

"Yes. But keep it to yourself. That's an order. The last thing we need right now is to start a panic."

"Of course, sir."

Devon exited the medical bay and headed down the corridor toward the Governor's office with Maya in tow.

"Devon?"

He did not answer, his mind distracted by a thousand thoughts at once.

"Devon?" This time she clutched his arm to catch his attention.

He paused and faced her. "What?"

"How are we going to stop that many people from overrunning the facility?"

"That's the problem. We can't."

CHAPTER TWENTY-FOUR

PETERSON MADE HIS way through the chaos of the surface-level elevator bay. Hundreds of citizens packed the domed structure, waiting for the long march to USC7 to begin. They had a charged energy, which was only natural since these were the most loyal followers of Caesar, the ones who believed most fervently in him. The ones who accepted the concept that USC7 was rightfully theirs. The ones devoted to this suicidal campaign. And sadly, the ones who would carry out his reign of terror on the innocents inside USC7.

Something did not settle right with Peterson. He wrote it off to the heat and humidity generated by so many bodies that hung heavily in the bay, only occasionally being relieved by a blast of frozen air blowing in from outside. Peterson sweated beneath his thermal clothes. He inhaled deeply when he reached the front of the crowd. The fresh air and freezing temperature felt good.

Caesar stood atop a Hagglund parked across the entrance to the bay, basking in his glory like his Imperial Roman namesake. A psychotic look shimmered in his eyes. Peterson assumed it must be the same glare a serial killer had when murdering his victims. Caesar wore his thermal coat but left it unzipped with the hood pulled down around his neck, a grand gesture showing his followers that the elements would not stop them. He clutched a microphone in his right hand. Raising it to his lips, Caesar turned it on. A squelch sounded through the bay and the speakers inside the facility.

"Citizens of New Empire, today marks a grand moment,

one that will go down in the annals of history. The negligence of our forefathers forced us to live underground these past thirty years, but that doesn't mean our empire can't expand. Today we march on USC7 and force them to share what we have been denied for so long. We will take over USC7, use its resources to build our empire, and, on the day when we can finally return to Above Earth, will be prepared to spread our influence over this country. The United States will once again reign supreme, not as a corrupt republic, but as an empire as vast and powerful as those of Alexander, Rome, and Constantinople."

Those inside the bay raised their fists above their heads three times, chanting, "Caesar! Caesar! Caesar!"

"Citizens of New Empire, let us march on USC7."

Like his namesake, Caesar had crossed his Rubicon.

The Hagglund pulled away from the exit and parked to the side, Caesar still standing on its roof. The citizens marched out in rows of five, ascending the slope. As they passed, each balled their right hands into a fist, tapped it against their chests three times, then extended their arm at a forty-five-degree angle. The idolized leader returned the gesture. As the first several hundred passed, the elevators descended to bring more citizens to the surface.

Peterson approached Caesar as he climbed down from the Hagglund. Caesar zipped up his coat and pulled the hood over his head.

"And so it begins, my friend."

"May your efforts be successful, sir." Peterson refused to consider the consequences of failure, which a sixth sense warned him would be imminent.

"Like any good leader, my place is at the head of my army. I'm taking one of the Hagglunds and will command from the front. The second Hagglund will follow later, protecting the ranks. You take the rear once everyone has left the facility and round up stragglers. I know I can count on you."

"Yes, sir."

"It's Caesar."

Peterson snapped to attention but refused to offer a salute. "Yes, Caesar. You can rely on me."

Caesar patted him on the shoulder and climbed into the passenger seat of the Hagglund. The driver pulled away, heading for the front of the column.

Peterson walked back inside the bay. The elevators returned with several hundred citizens, also die-hard followers who rushed out into the snow and fell in with the rest. The same with the third group. They charged off and followed the footsteps left in the snow, yelling at the top of their lungs to warn their comrades they would soon be joining them. The second Hagglund departed and fell in behind them.

Peterson noticed that none of the defense force personnel joined them. He asked himself where they were when the arrival of the fourth elevator answered that question.

None of these people were loyalists fanatically dedicated to their leader and this insane conquest. The fourth set of elevators comprised families, the elderly, and regular people who had survived thirty years of Hell and were now forced to join the others. They bore expressions of fear and resignation.

What had unsettled Peterson earlier suddenly dawned on him, making his blood run cold and churning his stomach. There were only fifteen hundred cold-weather suits throughout the facility. Like the three groups before them, none of these people had the proper clothing to make the trek to USC7. They had jury-rigged their attire as best they could. The lucky ones dressed in leather ponchos made from the hides of the remaining livestock slaughtered over the last few days. Others wore multiple layers of clothing, which would have minimal impact against the sub-zero temperatures. Some had cardboard and paper shoved under their clothes in a pathetic attempt at insulation. Very few owned hats, instead using blankets or spare clothing to drape around their heads. None had proper footgear. The smart ones had wrapped several layers of cloth around their feet and tied them in place with rope. Mothers swaddled babies in multiple blankets. No one donned sunglasses.

The defense forces that accompanied each group were fully adorned in cold-weather gear, but even they would be vulnerable to the elements for so long. It was one hundred and eighty miles to USC7, a seven-day journey. Few of these people would make it to the facility, and those who did would be in no shape to fight. For them, it would be a death march, Caesar's attempt to weed out the weakest.

Peterson turned when the elevators arrived for the fifth time, unable to watch this nightmare. He rummaged through the lockers, pretending to look for anything of use left behind. Instead, Peterson berated himself. He had allowed himself to become part of this massacre. Ostensibly, Peterson would bring up the rear to help stragglers along. There would be no stragglers. It would be a miracle if the defense force personnel survived, let alone the civilians. How could he have been so fucking stupid?

No, not stupidity. For years, Peterson had coped with the reign of terror by refusing to consider the consequences of the orders he carried out in Caesar's name. He never bothered to learn the names of those condemned to execution. Never followed up to discover how the redistribution of supplies, work assignments, or living quarters impacted the civilians. Never enquired about their quality of life. Peterson protected his conscience from guilt by turning a blind eye. Not anymore. He now watched everyone he had sworn to protect march off to certain death.

Peterson rode one of the elevators down to the sub-basement level to tour the facility one final time. He passed files of citizens, each waiting like death row inmates for their sentence to be carried out. One man argued with three defense force personnel, saying his wife had asthma and would not survive. When he refused to move, the personnel beat him unconscious, then forced the wife onto the elevators.

Making his way to the top level, he wandered the silent corridors. The power remained on but, with no one manning the reactors, a complete shutdown was inevitable. Roaches and rats had already taken over the abandoned areas. They scurried past him, no longer afraid of humans. He wondered what this place would look like in a few months, not that he would ever be coming back.

Farther along Ring D, a door opened and a child stuck her head out. Her mother yanked her back and closed the door. He heard the mother scolding the girl, saying now they would be forced to leave. Peterson pretended not to notice. It made sense that some citizens would opt to stay behind and try and make it on their own. Life would be miserable down here amongst the vermin, though still preferable to what the others faced.

He stopped by his suite. Opening the bottom drawer of his desk, he removed a photograph he had kept hidden all these years, a photo of his family during better times. Caesar murdered his parents and turned his beloved sister into a whore for the emperor's pleasure and humiliation. His parents would be ashamed of what he had become. He felt certain even his sister harbored a bitter hatred toward him. Why not? Peterson felt nothing but contempt for himself. Placing the picture on the desk, a small and pathetic act of defiance, he left the room and returned to the bay.

Peterson made it back in time to join the last group riding to the surface. He made his way to the rear, ignoring the hateful glares the citizens cast in his direction. When the elevator reached Above Earth, he stayed on it, watching the last citizens of New Empire shuffle off to their demise.

When the civilians had left, the remaining defense force personnel swarmed to the exterior walls of the bay and planted explosives. Peterson walked over to the closest soldier.

"What are you doing?"

"Following Caesar's orders. He told us to destroy the facility once everyone is gone."

Shit. Peterson slipped on his coat and ran out to the last Hagglund. Climbing into the vehicle, he pushed past the driver and ripped the microphone from its mount.

"Caesar, this is Peterson. Can you hear me?"

A frustrated voice answered. "Is there a problem?"

"Did you give orders to destroy the facility?"

"You have a lot to learn about history, my friend. When Cortez arrived in the New World, he burned his ships to give his men incentive to set up a new colony. I'm doing the same."

"What if we fail?"

"Failure is not an option." Caesar's voice had a tone as cold as the outside air. "I trust you will carry out my orders."

"Of course, Caesar. I'll oversee it myself."

"I know you will. You have great things ahead for you. Don't ruin it."

Peterson remained in the Hagglund, occasionally glancing out the window to check on the team's progress. After several minutes, they emerged from the bay. Most climbed onto snowmobiles and set off to run herd on the human cattle drive. The team leader, a man named Blade who also served as Caesar's executioner, raced over to the Hagglund, unrolling a spool of cable behind him. He crawled into the back of the vehicle. Cutting the cable and separating the two ends, he attached them to the detonator and passed it to Peterson.

"Here you go, sir."

"What's this for?"

"Caesar's orders. You're to have the honor of destroying New Empire."

Peterson took the detonator. One more indignity to add to his long list of shame. He ignited the explosives.

A muffled rumble came from inside the bay. Cracks formed on the top ice covering the dome, widening and multiplying. In seconds, the concrete structure collapsed. A cloud of dust rose from the debris, quickly being dispersed by the wind. A mound of rubble and ice sat where the bay had stood moments before, sealing off the main entrance to the facility.

Abbott took the detonator. He disconnected the cable and threw it outside, then placed the device in the rear.

"We're ready when you are, sir."

Peterson tapped the driver and pointed to the tail end of the mass of civilians. The driver pulled away and fell in behind them, keeping pace.

Peterson never looked back at New Empire.

CHAPTER TWENTY-FIVE

M AYA WAITED FOR the briefing to begin, thankful for the momentary break from physical exertion. The past forty-eight hours had been exhausting. IDF personnel worked double shifts. They maintained their patrols to keep up the appearance of normalcy, then spent another two four-hour shifts outside helping to build the Kill Zone, as Denning had begun referring to the area in front of the main line of defense. The same held true for EDF personnel. Those not assisting in the construction of the zone manned one of three defensive perimeters set up to protect the bay—the first line of defense established west of the Kill Zone to slow the attack, the main line of defense a quarter of a mile from the bay and directly behind the Kill Zone, and a third directly in front of the bay to serve as a last stand.

The biggest problem arose in manning these positions. Due to the cold, EDF and IDF personnel could stay outside no longer than four hours, limiting those on duty to three hundred and thirty at any given time. If the attack came unannounced, they faced up to twenty-eight thousand attackers at odds of a thousand to one. The rest of the defense forces, except for the IDF personnel on duty inside the facility, bunked down on the lower level of the elevator bay to be deployed quickly. Even the other cadets joined the main units, their training being placed on hold so their numbers could bolster the defense forces.

Besides herself, those attending the briefings were Haskell and Jake Matthews, who had replaced Denning as head of the EDF, the other shift leaders, the commanders for each line of defense and their subordinates, twenty various defense force personnel, three engineers, and Devon.

Behind the podium stood a map of the potential combat areas drawn on a whiteboard. A circle sat in the center, representing the bay. To the left of the bay sat a mound of snow and ice plowed away from the bay doors following the Great Freeze to create the slope leading topside. Over the decades, the mound had grown until it measured a thousand feet in circumference and over one hundred feet in height, providing a perfect defensive position. Off to the right, the wind had blown snow into a miniature mountain a thousand feet high and sloped on either side, which stretched a mile to the north, an insurmountable barrier. In between sat the Kill Zone, marked as such on the map, an area a thousand yards wide and a thousand feet long, the main defense they had against the invasion. A row of X's marked the locations of the three defense lines.

With advance warning of the assault and a large amount of luck, they might be able to stop the invasion.

Might.

It was a long shot.

Denning stood. He examined those in the room, stopping when he reached Maya. His eyes crinkled.

Devon spoke first. "Maya has been working with me on interrogating the prisoners and is privy to everything going on. Her input is valuable."

"Fair enough," replied Denning. Then, to Maya, "Cadet, don't be afraid to speak your mind."

"I will, sir."

"Preparations are set to repel the invasion. You've all been briefed on the situation and the defense plans. This is a final run-through to see if we missed anything. Now's the time to speak up if you see any flaws."

"How about the fact that we're dealing with odds of almost thirty to one?" asked Haskell.

Denning cut him a withering look but said nothing.

Devon jumped in. "Don't worry about the numbers."

"Do you know something we don't?" asked Williams.

"No. The prisoner told us twenty-eight thousand people lived at USC5 and would be forced to march to attack us. If you think in those terms, we don't stand a chance. However, bear in mind, between the Carbines and their pistols, they only have two thousand weapons, the same amount we do. The others will be attacking with hand-held weapons at best. That narrows the odds considerably. Most of that number are civilians with no combat training, including women and children. They'll break and run when the battle begins. Add to that, they have a seven-day journey from USC5. A good number will die of exposure before they even get here. Those who do survive will be exhausted. All of this gives us an advantage."

"What would you assess the odds at?" asked Haskell.

Devon did a quick mental calculation. "At worst, fifteen to one."

The general shook his head. "Those odds still suck."

"It's a lot better than the original assessment," added Matthews with a hint of optimism.

"That's what the Kill Zone is for. If we can take out a lot of them with one blow, it might encourage the rest to retreat."

"Getting off topic slightly," said one of the shift leaders, a middle-aged woman Maya had seen on numerous occasions but had never learned her name. "Are the citizens inside the facility aware of what's going on? Can we use them as a reserve in case the attackers break through?"

"To answer your first question, no." Some of the officers started to protest, but Denning cut them off. "It was a mutual decision by the Governor and me, with the approval of Haskell and Matthews."

"You're keeping everyone in the dark until the battle breaks out?" barked the middle-aged officer.

"Once the attackers are in the area, we'll notify everyone of the situation and tell them to shelter in place until it's over. Except for a few armed stragglers during the first few months of the Great Freeze who tried to fight their way in and the occasional attack by polar bears, we've lived in peace for thirty years. We have no idea how our people will react. Some may try to leave. Others may protest what we plan on doing. We can't afford to deploy forces to calm any social unrest, especially with the odds stacked against us.

"To answer your second question, our people aren't ready to engage in combat. We assume the enemy has a fighting force of between one and two thousand armed personnel, depending on how they distribute their weapons. We also assume that Caesar has a force of thugs, probably armed with close-in-combat weapons. What we don't know is the ratio between fanatical followers and civilians coerced to participate. A lot depends on that equation. If the only ones that break through are desperate civilians trying to survive, we can call on the citizens to help contain them. If the main force overwhelms us and gets inside, calling out the citizens to help will only result in their being slaughtered."

Devon jumped in. "Add to that the consideration that if our people try to stop the invasion and fail, we give Caesar a reason to brutalize those who survive. The Governor based her decision on what she felt best met the safety of everyone inside."

The protests came to an end.

"Any more questions?" asked Denning.

"I have one," said Maya as she leaned forward and studied the map. "What's at the eastern end of the Kill Zone?"

"The main line of defense."

"I mean between that and the end of the zone."

"Nothing. Why?"

"My guess is that with so many people at his disposal, Caesar will attempt a swarm attack on the facility."

"We assume the same. What's your point?"

"With nothing to slow them down, only a portion of Caesar's people will be on the Kill Zone when we initiate our plan. I suggest building a trench at the end of the zone, something that will slow down the advance and create a pile-up of people so the casualties are much greater."

Denning stared at Maya. For a moment, she thought she would get her ass chewed for talking out of turn. Then the commander turned to Haskell and Matthews.

"Can it be done?"

"I don't see why not." Haskell hesitated as he formed the plan in his head. "We should have enough time to build a sloping trench leading to a ten-foot wall. That'll slow them down considerably and create a mass over the Kill Zone."

Denning contemplated the plan for a few seconds. "It's settled. Haskell and Williams will oversee the digging of the trench."

"I have a question." One of the shift leaders, an Asian man named Yamamoto, spoke up. "Have we considered the possibility Caesar may attack in another direction or may use a diversionary attack? If they have explosives like we do, couldn't they breach the bay from behind?"

"It's possible but not probable. They would have to blast their way through so much ice we'd have plenty of time to launch a counter-offensive. In any case, we have guards posted along the top of the dome to warn us of any movement from another direction."

Yamamoto bowed his head.

There were no other questions.

"It's settled," said Denning. "You all know what to do. As of today, I'm extending the patrols in front of the base out to five miles. Hopefully, we'll have enough warning about the impending invasion so we're not caught by surprise. Dismissed."

Denning made his way over to Maya and Devon. "Cadet."

Maya snapped to attention. "Yes, sir."

"Excellent call back there about the trench." Then, to Devon. "You should be proud of her. She's a vital part of our forces."

"I am." Devon saluted. "Thank you, sir."

As the general left, Devon reached out and squeezed her hand. "Honestly, you came up with a great idea."

"Thanks." Maya blushed. "I can't believe I thought of a way to kill thousands of people."

"Stop thinking that way," he admonished her tenderly. "You thought of a way that may save us from being overrun, saving the lives of two hundred thousand innocent citizens. I'm proud of you. You should be, too."

"I guess." The way Devon explained it made her plan seem more acceptable. She still had a lot to learn about being a soldier.

"Come on. We need to go topside and help with digging the trench. But first…." Devon slid his hand into hers. "Why don't we go back to my quarters for a little R&R?"

Maya beamed. "I'd like that."

CHAPTER TWENTY-SIX

PETERSON RODE IN the passenger seat of the Hagglund, staring out the side window as they pulled into camp. He felt numb. Not from the cold. The heater inside the vehicle kept the compartment comfortable. The numbness, which dulled his emotions, resulting from the carnage he had witnessed the past four days.

It began three hours after leaving New Empire. The first victims were an elderly man and woman who had given up, lying down in the snow side by side and letting the cold suck from them what little life they had left. By the time the Hagglund had driven by, their bodies were frozen solid, their skin crystallized with ice. Peterson knew that not everyone would survive the march. He never expected to see the first fatalities so quickly.

They came across the next bodies a few miles later—a mother and her two young children. All three knelt in the snow, the mother's arms clutching the kids tight against her chest, her cow-hide shawl wrapped tightly around them. The cold had frozen them into this position, an icy grave. The body count rose throughout that first day. By the time Peterson reached the camp Caesar had set up before dusk, he had counted three hundred and eighteen dead, all succumbing to the elements.

Camp proved even more deadly. At least moving provided some semblance of warmth during the march. At night, those few not assigned to a Hagglund were exposed to the elements, with not even sunlight to offer minimal comfort. Everyone huddled together in large masses, sharing body heat to keep warm. Some of the more humane groups allowed women, children, and the elderly inside the center where it was warmest while the men rotated shifts among the outer layers. For many groups, especially those run by Caesar's fanatics, it became survival of the cruelest, with the weakest members forming the protective layer. Three of the Hagglund drivers allowed people to huddle against their vehicles for warmth since the engines ran all night, which undoubtedly saved lives. One of the drivers, a young woman named Teresa, allowed small children and mothers with babies to sit in shifts inside the compartment. These small shards of humanity, while appreciated, were far from enough. When the column marched off at dawn, Peterson had counted five hundred and eighty-three who had passed away that first night.

Day two of the trek proved far worse, with one thousand six hundred and forty-seven falling along the trail. Several carcasses had been ravaged by polar bears before the bodies froze, but hopefully after they died. Peterson noticed a few bodies, some alone and some in small groups, including children, lying face down and farther away from the trail with frozen bloodstains on their back. He assumed them to be deserters opting for a minimal chance of survival in the wilderness rather than face certain death in combat. Caesar had ordered his troops to execute anyone attempting to head out on their own. Maybe a few escaped and would make it, though Peterson seriously doubted it.

He stopped counting bodies an hour before dusk when the toll reached twenty-five hundred. Another three thousand died overnight.

Yesterday and today were the most brutal. In addition to death by the elements and execution, polar bears had begun attacking the column. If defense force personnel were near, they stopped the attacks. Sometimes. Those sections left defenseless had to fend for themselves with predictable results.

Ravaged bodies littered the trail in increasing numbers. Peterson had no idea how many people had been eaten alive. He had stopped counting bodies at the beginning of day three but estimated the death count between eight and ten thousand for the past two days.

Peterson had not witnessed this much death and bloodshed since the revolution that brought Caesar to power. Back in those days, it barely bothered him. Now it made him nauseous.

The Hagglund parked at the rear of the camp. Hundreds of citizens swarmed the vehicle, fighting to get near the engines and the life-saving warmth they provided. Peterson turned away, unable to watch as the people he lived with for thirty years were degraded into animals. He pulled the knit wool cap over his eyes and slumped down in his seat, hoping to get some sleep.

Jesse, the driver, reached into a cooler and removed a ration pack. He lightly tapped Peterson on the shoulder. The latter pushed up the cap onto his forehead.

"You want something to eat?"

Peterson shook his head and pulled down the cap.

From the back seat, Renee suggested, "Maybe we could share some of the food with the others."

"You mean those hovering around us?" asked TC, who sat behind Peterson. He had not washed in weeks and the compartment reeked of his stench.

"Yeah."

TC huffed in frustration. "We have three extra ration packs to share among several hundred people. How fucking stupid can you be? Are you trying to start a riot?"

No." Renee bowed her head. "I only want to help."

"That will only cause more problems than it'll solve." TC grabbed a ration bag and leaned against his seat, mumbling, "Dumb bitch."

Jesse shifted to look at Renee. "The only thing we can do to help these people is take USC7 as quickly as possible. Once it's ours, we can get everyone inside and start over."

TC massaged his crotch. "I'm looking forward to some of that fresh, new pussy we'll find there. You bitches are too old and used to be much fun anymore."

"That's enough!" Peterson never raised his wool cap. "TC, keep your dick in your pants until after we've taken the facility and leave Renee alone. All of you, shut up. I'm trying to—"

A commotion outside interrupted him. Peterson whipped off his cap and peered out. Crusher, one of Caesar's personnel bodyguards, made his way through the crowd circling the vehicle. Caesar had chosen Crusher both for his size, six-foot-three and over two hundred pounds of muscle, and his cruelty. The bodyguard displayed the latter trait by shoving people out of the way as he headed for the passenger door.

Shit, thought Peterson. *I'm never going to get any rest.* He opened the door, allowing a blast of frigid air inside. At least it dissipated the stench from TC.

"What do you need?"

"Caesar asked me to get you."

"Is everything okay?"

Crusher shrugged. "I guess. He didn't seem upset."

"Hang on."

Peterson zipped up his coat, slid on his hat and gloves, and climbed out. A young woman clutching a swaddled infant to her chest glanced at him. She nestled between the tracks and the road wheels, trying to stay out of the biting wind. Peterson helped her off the ice and ushered her inside the compartment.

"Wh-what are you doing?" she asked.

"Take my seat until I get back. It'll give you and your baby a chance to warm up."

Once she had sat down, thanking him repeatedly, Peterson closed the door and followed Crusher across the exposed compound to Caesar's vehicle. The group spread out over a square mile, with most people swarming around the Hagglunds for warmth or huddled together like a waddle of penguins.

Caesar had chosen a slight rise in the landscape to set up camp, providing a tactical advantage but exposing everyone to the wind. More people would die of exposure tonight than needed to.

Caesar's bodyguards prevented anyone from crowding around his Hagglund for warmth. As Crusher and Peterson approached, the guard by the passenger door knocked three times then opened it. Peterson climbed inside. Caesar sat in the back along with Charlotte and Maxine, eating from ration pouches. Charlotte smiled at her brother. Caesar placed the pouch between him and Maxine and wiped his hands on his coat.

"We're more than halfway there, my friend. Soon, all this will be behind us, and we'll set up the empire we deserve."

Peterson ignored the grandiosity. "The sooner we arrive, the better. We're losing a lot of people on this journey."

"How many?" Caesar asked without emotion.

"Ten thousand, maybe a little more."

"I expected the numbers to be higher. No loss, though."

Caesar's callousness caught Peterson off guard. "You realize we lost a third of our group in four days?"

"The weakest third. The ones that don't matter."

Peterson had no idea how to respond.

Caesar reached into the pouch, removed a slice of jerky, and stuffed it into his mouth. "We're culling the weakest from the pack, the ones who were the biggest burden in New Empire and would continue to be a burden. It's one of the reasons I destroyed our old facility. Those who died out here would have stayed behind and died even slower deaths as they starved. At least now they have a chance to claim some of the glory that will be Imperial Boston."

Peterson cocked an eye at the name.

"I originally thought of calling it New Rome, but their days of glory are long past. Our days of glory are only beginning."

"It's catchy."

Caesar leaned closer. "I know you disagree with my plan. And I understand. You view everyone out there as individuals, as having value. You must understand that I view those people as a group, the same way world leaders viewed their citizens as a country. It doesn't mean I don't care about them, but things have changed since the Great Freeze. I don't have the luxury of taxing those who work hard to support those who don't. If I left them behind, we would still be responsible for them and would either need to figure out a way to safely bring them to Imperial Boston or constantly supply them with our hard-won resources. I settled that problem by bringing them with us. The weak will perish and those who survive will earn their right to sit at the table with the rest of us."

Caesar pulled out another slice of jerky, pointing it at Peterson as if he were lecturing a class. "Survival is my main concern, not just for our people but for the country. There must be other facilities like ours in need of leadership. We'll find them, bring them under our control, and rebuild this country the way it should be. Once we have the new regime in place and secure, we can concentrate on luxuries such as arts and education. That's where you come in. When we get to USC7, I don't want you to stay behind."

"I thought you wanted me to lead the main assault." Peterson tried not to sound nervous.

"You're too valuable to lose in combat. Let the team leaders make the tactical decisions. You command from the rear."

"Does this mean I've lost your confidence?"

"The opposite. I'm trusting you to protect my most valuable possessions, Charlotte and Maxine."

Peterson bristled at hearing his sister called a possession.

"Charlotte and Maxine will help me bear the beginning of a long line of successors that'll ensure Imperial Boston remains strong for generations. I know you'll do anything to protect your sister. And I'm certain you'll do the same for Maxine."

"You have my word."

"Good." Caesar moved forward in his seat and placed a hand on Peterson's shoulder. "What we're doing now is difficult, but we must do it to survive. No one remembers the blood spilled and the people crushed to create great empires, only their legacies. This will all be over soon, and then we can forge a new way of life."

Peterson placed his hand on Caesar's and squeezed, more to ensure his survival than to show his support. "You can count on me."

"I know I can. Now go get some rest."

Peterson exited the compartment, winking at his sister before leaving, and made his way back to his Hagglund. He tried to wrap his mind around Caesar's rantings. The man wasn't only trying to take over one facility but the entire country and replace it with a dynasty. Insanity. And yet, in this new world, it could succeed.

CHAPTER TWENTY-SEVEN

DESPITE THE INEVITABLE, futile battle they faced, the last three days had been special for Maya because she and Devon had been able to share intimate moments. Only it had not been the tender lovemaking she had grown accustomed to. The time they spent in bed consisted of raw fucking, rough sex between two lovers experiencing the most out of life in the little time they had left. The good girl inside Maya was appalled at the things they had done. The bad girl fondly remembered everything. As Devon went to the bathroom to prepare for their shift, Maya replayed the last three nights in her mind.

Maya knew she needed to release the bad girl in all aspects of her life. She had changed considerably in the last seven weeks. The day she joined the EDF, she had been a wide-eyed cadet excited to serve society and do her part to make the end of the world bearable. That vision soon collapsed. She had been disillusioned at the dark undertones that streaked the utopian vision and even more appalled at Devon's role in it all. That self-righteous attitude fell away quickly when she realized the dangers they faced. At first, Maya felt like an idiot for believing the falsehoods the government fed her all her life. Only now did she realize the government protected the citizens from the truth so they could live their lives peacefully while a small handful dealt with the harsh realities everyone faced.

Maya saw that dual aspect in Devon, loving and tender in his private life yet calculating and determined the moment he slipped on his uniform. It unsettled her in the beginning until she understood what the enemy was capable of. Anger and contempt quickly morphed into respect as she realized that Devon took on this job not to satisfy some twisted whim but to protect the safety of the facility and the lives of two hundred thousand citizens. Maya realized he had pulled into this world so she could experience what he did, partially to understand him better, but also with the hope she would want to join it. To her surprise, she did.

However, for Maya to do that, she needed to cast aside her preconceived notions of right and wrong. She could no longer view the enemy's death as the taking of human lives but the prevention of having the same fate befall every citizen of USC7 as did the ambushed EDF patrol. Maya felt confident she could do it. Well, at least she hoped she could. It would be difficult to alter twenty-one years of conditioning, but she would have to do it if she wanted to survive the next few days.

Maya heard the shower come on in the bathroom. Swinging her legs out of bed and shedding her nightgown, she joined Devon.

✦ ✦ ✦

MAYA AND DEVON reached the lower level of the elevator bay thirty minutes before shift change. As they entered, a blast of cold air greeted them from the open door several levels above. Roma and Denning stood in the center of the bay, the former briefing the latter. Devon joined them, with Maya in tow.

"Did I miss anything?" he asked.

"No," Roma replied. "Everything's in place. We completed the trench in front of the main defense line early this morning. Our patrols still haven't spotted any sign of the invasion force."

"Maybe they all died on the march," added Denning.

Roma chuckled. "We can only hope."

"I wouldn't count on it," said Devon. "The best we can hope for is that the force will be significantly diminished and exhausted by the time it gets here."

"I know. I know." Denning frowned. "Plan for the worst, hope for the best."

"Yes, sir."

"The shift is yours," Roma said to Denning. "I'll stick around for another hour, then go catch some sleep. Good luck."

As the officers separated, Maya heard someone call her name. She turned around. The rest of the cadets stood at a nearby locker, changing into their cold-weather gear. She joined them.

Carver greeted her. Between his height and his padded clothing, he looked like a yeti. "It's good to see you. We had no idea what had happened to you."

"Yeah," said Medugno. "Byrd wouldn't tell us anything."

"That's Drill Instructor Byrd, sewer roach," Byrd said from behind them. "And that's because it's none of your damn business."

They all snapped to attention. Byrd stepped over to Maya. "I heard you're doing good things, cadet."

"I'm doing my best, sir."

"You should be proud of yourself." Then, to the others. "You have fifteen minutes to meet me topside. We're manning the forward defense line."

"Yes, sir," they all bellowed.

Byrd walked over to one of the elevators and rode it to Above Earth.

Bettany waited until the drill instructor stepped out of earshot. "Fill us in. What's going on?"

At first, Maya hesitated, not sure how much of what she knew was classified. Then she figured the more they knew, the better prepared they'd be. She relayed all the information she had gathered over the past few days. She left out how they had collected the intelligence from Jimmy. The others looked dumbstruck.

"Are you saying women and children are in the attack

force?" asked Sanchez.

"Probably not in the main wave. But they're somewhere in the column."

Bodman shook his head. "I can't kill women and children."

"You can and you will," snapped Maya, surprised at her own intensity. "I know what these people are capable of. They'll brutalize the women and kill off anyone who doesn't support them with those of us from the defense forces being first."

"Calm down," said Nori.

"This isn't the time to be calm. We're about to engage in a fight for our lives. These people are animals. It's us or them. I'll do whatever it takes to prevent my family from being slaughtered."

The other cadets stared at her. Carver spoke first.

"She's right. My great-great-grandfather fought in Vietnam. Granddad used to tell me stories about what he and his buddies had to go through to survive. If they did it, so can we."

A murmur of consent went through the others.

"I hate to be rude," said Medugno. "But if we're not topside on time, Byrd will chew our asses, even though the padded cloths."

"Good luck, guys."

"Where will you be?" asked Carver.

"I'll be up there with Devon. We're in charge of the Kill Zone."

"Oh, fuck," said Bettany. "You have the shittiest job."

"Tell me about it." Maya hugged her friend and whispered in her ear. "Take care of yourself."

"I will. Promise."

Maya left her friends and joined Devon on the other side of the bay to change into her winter gear. She hated being hard on them, but Devon had whipped her into shape. Besides, maybe Denning was correct. With luck, the enemy died on the journey from USC5.

CHAPTER TWENTY-EIGHT

"**S**IR," SAID GUTIERREZ, the driver. "There's a Hagglund up ahead."

Caesar woke from his nap and stared out the windshield. Another vehicle parked across their path a quarter of a mile away.

"Is it ours or theirs?"

"I can't tell, sir."

"Call up the snowmobiles in case we need to take it out."

Gutierrez removed the microphone from its mount and called the closest snowmobiles to move forward.

The Hagglund did not move. When Caesar's vehicle approached within three hundred feet, the driver's door opened and a figure stepped out onto the ice. He did not carry a weapon. Instead, he waved to get their attention. Caesar recognized him as Beast.

Gutierrez flashed the lights three times and Beast came forward. The two snowmobiles arrived and approached, high-fiving their comrade when they realized the other Hagglund posed no threat.

"Wait here." Caesar climbed out and made his way to Beast.

"Is there a problem?"

"No, sir. We're here to welcome you." Beast pointed to an icy slope two hundred feet ahead of them. "USC7 is just over the rise."

"Show me."

The two men walked up the slope, stopping at the crest.

A mile away at the base of the slope stood their destination—USC7. Lights from inside the open bay flowed out, illuminating the activity that went on topside. From the outside, it looked exactly like New Empire, the domed roof of the upper bay covered in hundreds of feet of snow and ice. They had made it. Two miles away sat salvation, with plenty of food and resources to give his people the fresh start they deserved. Within twenty-four hours, he would be inside, the new leader of what would become Imperial Boston. Then he would weed out the malcontents and those who could not be trusted. Once the survivors had recovered from the trek and those left alive inside had fallen into line, he could begin rebuilding America under his control and let it rise to glory that, by rights, it should be.

"Isn't it beautiful, sir?"

"It is. It'll be a new beginning for us." Caesar stared at the facility. "What have you learned about their defenses?"

"They're relying mostly on the two mounds of ice on either side of the entrance. The one on the left has an icy cliff and is insurmountable. The one on the right is easy to take, although they do have defensive positions on top. The best option is a straight run down the center. They set up foxholes in front of the mounds and a trench on the other side, but that's for their troops to fight from rather than stop us."

Caesar smiled. This would be easier than he had anticipated. "Good job, Beast."

"Thank you, sir. What now?"

"Tonight, we rest. We'll attack at dawn."

CHAPTER TWENTY-NINE

"WHY DID YOU let Martin drive?" Elaine complained from the back seat, staring out at the blanket of white that engulfed their Hagglund.

"Because he needs the experience," replied Franklin, the team leader, from the passenger seat.

"Now we're lost."

"We're not lost," snapped Martin, his nervousness evident.

"Then where are we?"

"I don't know."

"So, we're lost."

"Can it, corporal." Franklin shifted in his seat to glare at Elaine. "He's learning to navigate on instruments, so cut him some slack. Besides, if I remember correctly, your first time driving, you went over a snow mound you thought was solid ice, and we spent three hours digging you out."

"Really?" chuckled Martin.

Franklin cast a disapproving glance at Martin. "Concentrate on getting us home."

"Yes, sir."

Elaine crossed her arms across her chest, a task made more difficult by the heavy winter clothing. Being lost didn't scare her. Each Hagglund had a GPS for navigation and a tracking device in case they broke down so the facility could locate them. She worried about being out here with an invasion force on the way. Nor did it help that Denning was wound as tight as a spring the past few days and jumped down everyone's throats for the slightest infraction. Elaine did not want to do double duty because Martin got them back to the facility late.

"Here's the turn." Martin veered the Hagglund to the right. "It's three miles to the bay."

"Good job," complimented Franklin. "I knew you could do it."

They drove for a few minutes before another Hagglund emerged from the snow.

"They must have sent out a search party for us," commented Martin.

"Not without trying to reach us by radio first." Franklin's tone had an edge to it.

Elaine leaned over to look out the side window. From what she could see through the storm, scores of people milled about, mostly civilians. A defense force soldier stepped away from the Hagglund and fired a warning shot in front of their vehicle.

"Shit. It's the invasion force." Franklin reached for the radio as Martin floored the accelerator to escape.

Seeing that the Hagglund did not obey, the defense force soldier fired again, this time at the side of their vehicle. Elaine dropped to the floor as eight bullets shattered the side glass and punctured the metal walls. Frigid air flowed in, dropping the inside temperature by twenty degrees. One round struck Franklin in the right temple, tearing off the left side of his head and splattering Martin. Franklin's body dropped between the two seats. To his credit, Martin did not flinch and kept on driving.

More bullets tore into the cab as the invaders attempted to stop them from escaping.

Elaine scrambled to the front, climbed over the corpse of her commanding officer, and pulled the microphone from its mount.

"USC7, this is Corporal Elaine Fyler of Team Two. We made contact with the enemy. They are approximately two miles from the bay. I repeat, this is Corporal Elaine Fyler of Team Two. We made contact with—"

Another burst of gunfire ripped through the Hagglund, this time shattering the windshield. Two bullets hit Martin in the chest and one in the head, killing him instantly. His body slumped forward onto the steering wheel. The Hagglund came to a stop.

As Elaine crawled in back for her Carbine, the front passenger door whipped open and one of Caesar's soldiers crawled inside. On seeing Elaine, he riddled her with four three-round bursts.

✧　✧　✧

CAESAR HAD BEEN napping in the passenger seat of the Hagglund when he heard a commotion outside. He raised his head in time to see a second vehicle making its way toward them. At first, he thought one of his commanders was coming to confer with him. One of his men fired a warning shot across its bow. The Hagglund sped up and tried to escape, only to be stopped within fifty feet by a hail of gunfire. A soldier climbed into the vehicle, fired at someone inside, then ran over to Caesar's vehicle.

Caesar opened his door, wincing against the blast of air. The soldier raced to the opening and pumped his chest three times.

"What's happened?"

"An enemy patrol stumbled on us. One of them radioed our presence to USC7."

Fuck! They had lost the element of surprise. Now he would have to rely on sheer numbers for the plan to succeed.

Peterson joined them from his Hagglund. "What's going on?"

"An enemy patrol reported our position to USC7."

"Shit."

"We're launching the attack now."

"In the middle of the night?" asked Peterson.

"I want to catch them off guard." Caesar turned to the soldier. "Spread the word we move out in five minutes."

"Yes, sir." The soldier ran off to inform the others.

Caesar focused his attention back on Peterson. "While I initiate Plan B, you're in charge here. Keep driving them until we're inside the facility. You know what to do."

"I do."

Caesar patted him on the shoulder. "Protect my girls."

Peterson had never heard Caesar affectionately refer to Charlotte and Maxine that way before. "You can count on me."

"I know I can. Now get going. We move out in three minutes."

CHAPTER THIRTY

IRV TUCKER LEANED back in his chair in front of his radio, one headphone covering his ear and the other resting on his temple. His eyes were closed, and he breathed slow and deep.

"Don't fall asleep on me." Brian MacDonald nudged Tucker in his right arm.

"I'm not. I'm resting my eyes." Tucker kept them closed. "Besides, it's not like we're being overwhelmed with comms. Other than the hourly check-in, it's been a quiet night."

"I don't want to be the one up all night while you nap."

Tucker opened his eyes and glanced around the comm room, a twenty-foot by twenty-foot space containing the external and internal communications for the facility. It also contained radio and TV equipment used to monitor public broadcasts from Above Earth that stopped transmitting thirty years ago. "Who's going to know? It's just us. So long as one of us is awake, it's fine. We can take turns if you want."

Brian shrugged. "I'm anxious to get this over with. I'm not used to these overnight shifts."

"Well, get used to them. We may be doing these for—"

The radio crackled and a frantic female voice came over the speaker.

USC7, this is Corporal Elaine Fyler of Team Two. We made contact with the enemy. They are approximately two miles from the bay. I repeat, this is Corporal Elaine Fyler of Team Two. We made contact with—

A burst of semi-automatic weapons fire cut off Elaine. Then the radio went silent.

The two men stared at each other for a second, allowing

the warning to sink in. Tucker tapped Brian on the shoulder and pointed to the phone on the console.

"Call the Governor and let her know what's going on, then try to reach Elaine again."

As Brian picked up the receiver, Tucker grabbed the microphone from its mount and pressed the talk button. "This is Sergeant Tucker. Get me General Denning. Now!"

✧   ✧   ✧

DEVON GLANCED AT his watch.

"Do you have a hot date?" asked Maya jokingly.

He flashed her a grin. "Later tonight I do."

"Keep it in your pants," chided Denning. "We have a job to do."

"Yes, sir."

The three of them stood at the open door to the bay, staring out over the defensive positions and the Kill Zone as they had been for hours, waiting for the inevitable. And hoping it would never happen.

"How close do you think they are?" asked Denning.

"Assuming they travel fifteen to twenty miles a day, they should be here anytime. Given the conditions, it's possible they could travel only ten miles a day, which means we might not see them for a week."

"What if they traveled more than twenty miles a day?"

"It's unlikely given the cold and ice. If Caesar's forces had, they would have arrived a few days ago."

"Shit," Denning mumbled under his breath. "The longer we wait, the more tired and stressed our people become."

Maya understood completely. Waiting only increased her anxiety. It had also given her time to play out various scenarios in her head, none of which worked out well for them. She almost preferred combat to—

Haskell ran up to them. "General, we heard from one of

our patrols. The invasion force is here. They're two miles in that direction." He pointed to the crest of the ice hill in front of the forward defense line.

A cold emptiness formed in the pit of Maya's stomach.

"Details."

"There are none. Corporal Fyler reported their position then went off the air. We think they were ambushed."

"Shit. Has the Governor been informed?"

"They're doing so now."

"Where's the last Hagglund?" asked the general.

"Still on patrol."

Denning mentally calculated his next course of action. It took only a few seconds.

"Haskell, gather up the reserves. Double the number of people manning the forward defense line and deploy the rest east of the Kill Zone."

The captain raced off.

Denning turned to Devon and Maya. "Get on the radio and inform everyone the enemy is here. Tell the lookouts on the dome to let us know if they spot an attack from another direction. Warn our unit on the hill to be ready for a possible flank attack. And tell the IDF personnel on duty inside the facility to be prepared in case the enemy breaches our defenses."

"What about the other Hagglund?" asked Maya.

"Where is it now?"

"To our south."

"Warn them what's going on. They can either stay where they are or try to sneak back. If they choose the latter, tell them to approach from the south. And be sure they warn us when they get close so we don't shoot them by accident."

"Roger that." Devon motioned for Maya to follow him.

The two set off to inform the other units.

Denning looked out over the defensive positions and the Kill Zone. *If these bastards want a fight, we'll make them pay dearly for it.*

✦ ✦ ✦

"THANK YOU," SAID Governor Mangerian as she stared blankly at the receiver. "Have Denning keep me informed of everything that happens."

She placed the phone back in its cradle and sighed. This must be how the people of Rome felt when the Goths approached the city. She only hoped that the defenders would be luckier this time.

Reaching across her desk, Governor Mangerian pulled toward her the microphone connected to the facility's speaker system and switched on the power button.

"Citizens of USC7, this is your Governor speaking. We're facing a crisis. USC7 is about to be attacked by a powerful enemy force that wants to take over our facility for themselves. It is imperative that no one panic. Let our defense forces handle the situation. Everyone who is currently in their quarters, please shelter in place. If you are on the night shift, please return to your quarters. The IDF personnel on duty will keep you safe. Again, I note that it is imperative no one panic. Stay in your quarters until the all-clear signal is issued.

"I won't lie to you. The situation is desperate. The enemy outnumbers us by as much as thirty to one. However, we have the advantage of our defensive positions, manned by a well-trained and dedicated defense force, each willing to lay down their lives for our safety. With courage, determination, and God's grace, we'll come through this crisis."

The Governor paused.

"Yes, I said with God's grace. I know most of us stopped being religious after the Great Freeze. Like me, I'm sure some of you still believe in a divine entity, although you keep your religious practices private. If you believe, pray for our defense forces and for victory. If you don't, now is a good time to start.

We need all the help we can get. I'll fill you in as the situation develops."

Governor Mangerian turned off the power and focused on the microphone. Several thoughts raced through her head at once. She hoped the citizens of USC7 would listen to her and shelter in place, for their own safety as well as those topside. She hoped the defense forces would be able to repel the invasion. And she hoped that a miracle would occur to prevent the facility from being breached and taken over by these barbarians. After viewing the bodies of the three EDF personnel brutalized by the enemy, the thought of that happening to the two hundred thousand citizens here depressed and infuriated her.

Opening the lower desk drawer, the Governor removed an old cigar box from under a pile of papers, placed it on the desk, and lifted the lid. Inside sat a .38 revolver her father had smuggled into the facility in case things did not go as planned and he needed to defend his family. Thankfully, back then his paranoia proved unfounded. Now she appreciated his foresight. If the facility fell, Mangerian refused to be taken alive, tortured, and most likely executed in front of her people to make an example out of her. She would lead by example.

There were six bullets in the revolver—five for any barbarians who entered the facility.

The last one for herself.

✧ ✧ ✧

FULL CAPTAIN PAK Soon-he stood in the western-most foxhole on the snow hill to the left flank of the bay. She scanned the horizon with binoculars.

"Will you knock it off?" complained Javan Fleming, who crouched beside her. "I told you, it was the wind."

"I know I heard gunfire," she replied, not taking her eyes off the ridge.

"Maybe one of our patrols is shooting polar bears. They should be returning anytime now."

"Then where are they?"

"Maybe they got eaten."

Soon-he glared down at him. "That's not funny."

He ignored her and cuddled his legs against the cold.

Soon-he went back to scanning the horizon with her binoculars. She knew she had heard gunfire. Maybe one of the patrols was shooting at polar bears. But what if it wasn't? She did not want to be overrun by—

Her radio squawked. "Major Pak, this is Lieutenant Williams. Do you read me?"

Soon-he removed the radio from her belt. "I'm here."

"We spotted the enemy a few minutes ago by one of our patrols."

Javan looked up at her, shock in his eyes.

She ignored him. "How many are we facing?"

"No clue. Gunfire cut off the report before we got any details. But be ready. The attack will occur any minute."

"Are we getting reinforcements?"

"They'll be there shortly."

"Roger that." Soon-he slid the radio back on her belt and turned to Javan. "I told you I heard gunfire."

"You win." Javan stood and stretched his cold, aching muscles. "What now?"

"Go warn the others the invasion is imminent. Tell them to get ready to kick some ass."

BYRD SAT IN the center foxhole on the forward defense line. He would never admit it to the cadets, but he was scared. Only an asshole wouldn't be. Sure, he had been part of the EDF for almost two decades before becoming a drill instructor, but had never seen combat or fired a weapon in anger, not even at a polar bear. Now he faced a ruthless enemy that knew no mercy. Byrd wondered how his cadets were faring. He prayed his training would pay off.

A noise from behind Byrd caught his attention. He spotted Haskell approaching, leading seventy-four EDF personnel with him. The soldiers each deployed to the foxholes. Haskell and another soldier ran up to him, the captain jumping in beside Byrd.

Byrd glanced at his watch. "Isn't it early for shift change?"

"I wish. The enemy is over that rise. They'll be attacking any minute."

Byrd felt his bowels clench.

Haskell pointed to the soldiers jumping into the foxholes around him. "These are our reinforcements. Robinson and I will take this foxhole. You double-up with whoever is beside us. If anything happens to me, you're in command."

"Yes, sir. Good luck."

Byrd climbed out of the foxhole, ran to the one to his right, and jumped in. Medugno stared at him, fear evident in his eyes.

"I assume we're not being replaced," said the cadet.

"Nope. The enemy is over the ridge and is about to attack."

Medugno pushed aside the fear, a look of confidence washing over his face. "So, we get to die gloriously while slowing down the enemy."

"Maybe we'll be lucky. If we're not, think of the songs future cadets will song about you."

Medugno smiled. "The Ballad of Butterfingers."

Byrd chuckled and tapped him on the shoulder. "Make me proud, cadet."

✧　✧　✧

DENNING ISSUED ORDERS in preparation for the attack when General Arasaki stepped up.

"Excuse me, General Denning."

"I don't have time to discuss the ethics of the Kill Zone with you."

"I'm not here for that." Arasaki snapped to attention. "I'm still a soldier in the defense force and want to fight alongside my men."

"You don't have to do this."

"I must, for my honor and the honor of the defense forces."

"Join the main defense line by the trench."

"As you wish, General." Arasaki saluted.

Denning extended his hand. "I'm honored to have you serve under me."

Arasaki took the hand is his and squeezed. "Thank you. May we both live to see another day."

As Arasaki rushed off to his position, Denning's chest swelled with pride for his former commander's sense of duty. Then he returned to the more immediate task at hand.

✧ ✧ ✧

CAESAR AND PETERSON stood by the former's Hagglund, looking out over the invasion force. If you could use the word force to describe the rag-tag group that gathered before them. Only thirteen thousand had survived the journey from New Empire. Luckily, that included the strongest and most determined, those willing to die for the cause and capable of fighting for it. That number included the entire one-thousand-man defense force, the three thousand citizens most fanatical to the cause, as well as an additional two thousand who became devoted followers during the week-long march.

"I hope we have enough people," said Peterson. "We lost fifteen thousand getting here."

"Have faith." Caesar beamed with pride. "We have six thousand fighting men and women, more than enough to overwhelm the facility's defenses. And remember, those people are fighting merely to maintain their way of life. We're fighting for our survival."

Caesar climbed onto the top of his Hagglund and faced his army. They were strong and determined. And they knew there was no going back. Now to whip them into a frenzy.

"Citizens of New Empire," Caesar yelled over the roar of the wind blowing across the tundra. "Today marks the end of the miserable life we have led for so long and begins a new chapter of glory. Despite the odds, we have survived everything fate has thrown against us for the last thirty years. We did not make it this far because of luck. We made it this far because we are the chosen ones, the ones who will restore this country to the proud standing it once knew.

"And we achieved this while those people…" Caesar pointed toward USC7, "…lavished in a luxury we never knew. They never helped us. Never gave us supplies or assistance. They never even checked to see if we were alive. Their days of narcissism are over. Today we take what is rightfully ours. We will not waste it on our own selfishness. We will use what they have squandered to rebuild this nation and form a new and mighty empire."

The closest six thousand punched their chest three times and saluted. Those to the rear—the women, children, elderly, and the weak—stared at each other, uncertain of their fate.

"Give them no quarter! Show them no mercy!"

A roar rose from the army, and they charged off toward the facility. The thousand devoted followers armed with bladed weapons led the way, followed by the five thousand armed with melee weapons. They were the cannon fodder that would allow the eight hundred defense personnel to get close enough to the enemy to overwhelm the defenses. Fifty members of the defense forces followed to the rear, ensuring the rest of the group would participate in the fighting.

Three Hagglunds broke from the group, accompanied by one hundred defense force personnel, and headed for the snow hill that protected the facility's left flank.

As the forces crested the slope and charged the enemy's defense, Caesar faced Peterson. "It's time."

"Good luck, sir."

"Thank you." In an uncharacteristic gesture, Caesar hugged Peterson. "I'll see you inside."

Caesar walked over to the fifth Hagglund, one of the original four from New Empire outfitted with armor plates, and climbed in. Abbott started the engine and headed for the northern flank of USC7 with a hundred defense personnel in tow.

CHAPTER THIRTY-ONE

ASKELL HEARD THE battle cry come from the opposite
slide of the slope. The rest of the line also heard the roar,
each aiming their Carbines in that direction.

The first enemy soldiers crested the slope. They did not
wear cold-weather gear or carry the weapons typical of defense
force personnel. Haskell found it amazing they had made it this
far. They wore several layers of clothing, boots with cloth
wrapped around them, shirts as scarves and headgear. The
only weapons these people branded were knives and swords.
Yet they raced down the slope, screaming and thumping their
chests, charging the forward positions. Caesar had sent in his
crazed fanatics to clear the path. These people would not stop
until they were dead.

Haskell was happy to oblige.

"Fire!"

Hundreds of rounds slammed into the attackers, creating a
red mist. Gunfire cut down more than half the attackers
instantly. The survivors screamed louder and increased their
speed. Some of those cresting the top carried M17 semi-
automatic pistols and returned fire, their aim inaccurate.
Rounds ricocheted off the ice in front of Haskell's defense line
or passed harmlessly over the defenders' heads. A few bullets
found their mark. Up and down their positions, cries came
from those hit by stray rounds. Some of the wounded dropped
their weapons and screamed in agony. Others sucked it up and
maintained fire. The barrage continued.

More attackers fell, those behind jumping over the bodies

and continuing the charge. Several stopped to replace their melee weapons with the bladed weapons of their fallen comrades. For each one killed, several more took their place.

Then, inevitably, the gunfire lessened as the defenders reloaded.

The human tidal wave surged forward. The more competent attackers paused to steady their aim. They waited for the defenders to emerge from the foxholes, then took them out with shots to the head.

BYRD DUCKED DOWN to reload. Beside him, Medugno popped out the empty magazine and fumbled to insert a new one.

"Slow down and remember your training."

"Yes, sir."

Byrd stood and fired into the horde. A bullet slammed into the rim of his foxhole, throwing shards of ice into his sunglasses. He winced involuntarily and kept on firing three-round bursts at an attacker aiming at him. Two bullets tore into the attacker's chest, tearing apart his abdomen. He dropped the pistol and fell face-first onto the ice. A woman behind him bent down, scooped up the pistol, and kept firing. Byrd lowered his aim. Two shots ripped off her right leg while the third hit the left leg of a middle-aged man behind her. Both collapsed onto the ice. The others maneuvered around them.

Medugno jumped up and fired on full-automatic mode. Bullets ripped across the attackers, taken down five with strikes to the head and shoulders.

"Aim lower," suggested Byrd.

"We won't kill as many that way."

"The cold will kill them. We only need to stop them."

THREE FOXHOLES AWAY, Bettany and Sanchez maintained fire on the attackers who were now halfway down the slope.

Several tripped over the bodies or slipped on the blood but regained their footing and continued to advance, closing the distance with the forward positions.

CARVER AND BODMAN stood in the next foxhole. Carver ducked down to reload when Bodman fell beside him.

"Take it easy, man."

Bodman did not respond. A hole punctured his sunglasses. Carver pulled down Bodman's hood. The bullet had traveled through his skull and blew off the back of his head. A pile of brains and blood filled the hood, steaming from the cold.

Carver jumped up and resumed firing.

NORI FELT PANIC racing through him. He had expected the barrage would stop the assault. Despite the hail of gunfire, the attackers surged forward. Within minutes, the enemy would overrun them.

CAESAR'S DEFENSE FORCE personnel crested the ridge. The assault proceeded as planned. Scores of corpses and wounded dotted the slope, but they pushed forward. Now it was their turn.

Each soldier dropped to one knee, aimed carefully on the foxholes, and emptied a magazine into the defenders with devastating results.

FROM HIS POSITION on top of the snow hill, Javan observed the carnage in the valley below.

"Our people are getting slaughtered. We have to help them."

He started to climb out of his foxhole, but Soon-he pulled

him back.

"We have more important things to worry about."

"Like what?'

"That." She pointed to the three Hagglunds approaching the bottom of the hill with approximately thirty men hidden behind each vehicle.

She grabbed her radio and pressed the talk button. "This is it, people. Take out the Hagglunds first, then concentrate on the foot soldiers."

BEAST DROVE THE armor-plated Hagglund on the far left, waiting for the enemy to fire back. Not that it mattered. The longer it took them to fight back, the better the chances of completing his mission. He hoped his people would live long enough—

Several streams of gunfire slammed into his Hagglund and the one in front of him.

SERGEANT WATERS DROVE the Hagglund along the ice layer covering the dome to the USC7 bay.

"Maybe we should hang back," said Stephanie. "Brian said the attack would begin at any minute."

"All the more reason to haul ass. I don't want to be out here when the shit hits the fan. If we run into an enemy unit, we're screwed."

"You should listen to her, sarge," warned Thomson from the back. "We could wind up in the crossfire."

"Both of you, shut up. I know what I'm doing."

Waters agreed with them, but he had a greater priority than keeping his team safe. His wife and baby girl were trapped inside the facility. He refused to sit back and watch from the sidelines as—

Gunfire came from their left. Stephanie and Thomson

looked at each other and then at Waters. He ignored them, accelerating to full speed.

LIEUTENANT HESSMAN WATCHED the attack against the first defensive position through his binoculars on top of the dome above the bay doors. You didn't have to be a military strategist to know things were not going well. He had friends in those foxholes, including his brother.

"Should we help them?" The question came from Corporal Barrow, who shared the foxhole with him.

"They're too far away. We'll only waste ammo. All we can do is be ready to cover our people when they fall back."

"Yes, sir."

His radio squawked. He picked it up. "Hessman here."

"Sir, this Ionescu." She had watch over the northern sector of the dome. "We have enemy activity in Sector Four. A Hagglund followed by a hundred troops."

"Any chance it's our people?"

"Doubtful. It has the same markings as the one we lost several days ago."

Shit, thought Hessman. *That's all we need.* "Are they trying to outflank the bay?"

"Negative. It looks like they're heading for the northern sector of the dome."

"Inform Denning and keep me posted."

MAYA HAD PSYCHED herself for combat, but nothing could have prepared her for witnessing it first-hand. Even from the open bay doors, she could see the piles of bodies massing on the top of the slope and blood running down the ice, freezing into crimson rivulets. She considered the possibility they might not survive this attack.

"General Denning, this is Private Ionescu. Do you copy?"

The general keyed the talk button. "What's up?"

"We have an enemy column approaching the northern flank of the dome. One Hagglund and close to a hundred soldiers."

"Are they trying to outflank us?"

"I don't think so. They're heading away from our positions but staying close to the dome."

"Keep me posted." Denning slid the radio back onto his belt. "What the hell are they doing?"

"Deserters?" asked Maya.

"Doubtful." Denning thought for a moment. "What do we have in Sector Four?"

"Nothing." Devon shook his head. "That's where the nuclear reactor is located, but it's several hundred feet underground. They'd need a nuclear weapon to take it out."

The realization dawned on Maya. "The emergency exit."

Denning met her gaze. "What are you talking about?"

"The emergency stairwell leading from the sub-basement topside. You pointed it out on my first patrol."

Devon's eyes widened. "The path to the doorway is already dugout. All they'd have to do is blow the lock. Once they're inside the facility, it's over."

"Fuck." Denning calculated a new plan. "You and Cadet Santos go below. Round up the IDF personnel on duty inside the facility and stop those bastards. We can't let them get in behind us."

"Yes, sir. Good luck."

Maya had already broken into a run for the nearest elevator, waiting for Devon to catch up. She pressed the descent button and pulled off her cold-weather coat. A part of her wished she could warn her family.

PETERSON LEFT THE women in the Hagglund and made his way over to the slope, standing to one side to watch the battle.

Despite the carnage, their people surged ahead, gladly giving their lives for Caesar. The forward defensive line would be overwhelmed in minutes. Then they would face the more heavily defended second line. He tried to push from his mind the image of the coming slaughter.

"Get moving!" yelled a voice behind him.

"You can either die here or trying to take the facility," called out another voice. "Your choice."

Peterson turned around. The remaining defense forces were herding the rest of the group toward the slope, prodding the more reluctant with their Carbines.

CAESAR TAPPED ABBOTT on the shoulder. "Stop here."

The driver brought the Hagglund to a halt.

Caesar opened the door and stepped out into the ice. Two hundred feet in front of him stood the ice tunnel leading to the emergency exit built into all facilities. The fools had not only kept it open but left it unguarded, sealing their demise.

Semi-automatic fire came from the top of the dome. Several rounds slammed into the Hagglund above and to the right of Caesar. One defender fired at him from a foxhole dug into the top of the dome, the other aiming for his men. Five were killed or wounded in the initial attack. Then a fusillade of gunfire wracked the foxhole, neutralizing the threat. Caesar remained stoic, though inside he knew his close call with death signified victory would be his.

"Breach the door."

Crusher took four men and rushed forward, three providing cover fire as Crusher and the fourth raced down the ice tunnel. They attached C4 to the door handle and lock, set the primer, and quickly exited. Once they had taken cover on either side of the tunnel entrance, one of the men removed a detonator from his pocket and pressed a button. A muffled explosion sounded from inside the tunnel, followed a few seconds later by billowing smoke. Before the smoke cleared, Crusher led the soldiers back down the tunnel. One of them yelled, "All clear."

Caesar entered first, followed by the rest of his unit. The door lay ajar, having been blown off one of its hinges and shoved aside to make room. Three soldiers stood outside the doorway, saluting him as he passed. Crusher and the other soldiers stood on the inside landing, their Carbines trained down. Caesar moved to the railing and peered over the side.

A stairwell fifty feet square containing concrete-reinforced metal stairs descended two thousand feet to the sub-basement. Not a single person guarded the entry into the facility. This would be even easier than he had envisioned.

"Follow me."

Caesar unslung the Carbine from his shoulder and headed down the stairs, his men close behind him.

CHAPTER THIRTY-TWO

THE ATTACKERS CLOSED to within one hundred feet of the forward defense line. More than half their numbers lay dead or dying on the slope. The defenders shot frantically into those still alive, bringing down another fifty or so, but nowhere near enough to stop them.

A second horde topped the slope, three times larger than the first, comprised mainly of the elderly, women, and children. Soldiers with weapons prodded them to attack, yet the group paused, aghast at the bloodshed before them.

A boy barely ten years old broke away from his mother, rushed down the slope, and grabbed an ax off the ice. Brandishing it over his head, he screamed at the top of his lungs and charged. It broke the hesitation. Others ran forward, picked up whatever weapon they could find, and followed. Within seconds, another ten thousand people flowed down the slope, screaming and calling out, "Death to the enemy."

Haskell had only one option available. He emptied his magazine into the closest attackers, switched out the empty with a new one, and climbed out of the foxhole.

"Fall back!"

SEMI-AUTOMATIC FIRE TORE into the lead Hagglund of Beast's unit, the one commandeered days ago. Without armor plating, the rounds shredded those inside and killed a dozen soldiers following behind the vehicle. It ground to a halt, coming to rest at an angle. The remaining soldiers hid behind it and shot back at the defenders along the northern rim of the snow hill.

Bullets ricocheted off the armor plating of Beast's Hagglund. He kept on driving, heading for the eastern side. The soldiers huddled behind his vehicle spread out around him, half breaking to the left and falling prone, maintaining a stream of gunfire against the foxholes. The rest ran around the right flank and moved ahead, clearing a path. From the back, Cody and Kevin fired through the slits in the armor plating at the defenders.

Off to his right, the battle grew more intense. Beast peered out the slit in his right window in time to see two USC7 soldiers rushing toward the third Hagglund. The soldiers behind it attempted to take them down, being killed or scattered by concentrated fire from the foxholes along the opposite side. One of the USC7 soldiers died in a hail of bullets. The other, though wounded in the leg, hobbled toward his target, finally reaching the Hagglund.

An explosion rocked the hilltop, tearing apart the vehicle. Several of its armor plates blew off the sides and back, one of the latter slicing through the men behind it. Fire and thick black smoke billowed out of the holes ripped in its side. An engulfed in flames, a lone figure jumped out of the side door and ran, making it only a few yards before collapsing onto the ice.

Fuck, thought Beast. *These bastards are using suicide runners laced with C4 to stop them.*

He veered the Hagglund right, away from the foxholes.

SOON-HE FELT THE concussion rock the ground. She looked over the rim of the foxhole. The second Hagglund burned furiously.

"Two down," she mumbled to herself.

From the foxhole a hundred feet to their left, two USC7 soldiers jumped out, each holding a C4 bomb, and rushed the third vehicle, one from the left flank and the other from the front. The first suicide runner made it several yards before gunfire from the soldiers behind the vehicle cut him down. Two rounds shot off his right leg, and another pierced his abdomen. He fell to the ice, crawling toward his target. Another burst killed him.

The soldiers on the Hagglund's right flank ran forward and aimed at the second runner. Fifteen bullets tore into him, one striking the C4 bomb. It detonated. The explosion tore the runner apart, sending limbs and organs flying across the hilltop. Shrapnel killed two of the attackers.

"Fuck this." Javan crawled out of the foxhole and ran for the unexploded bomb. Soon-he covered him, bringing down three attackers. Javan made it ten feet before a bullet caught him in the hip. He crashed onto the ice, still crawling for the bomb. A string of automatic fire chewed across his back.

"Bastards!" Soon-he stood and emptied her magazine into the attacker who had killed Javan. She did not notice the two attackers sneaking up on her flank. She only felt the bullets tearing into her body before she died.

BEAST FLOORED THE Haglund and headed for the opposite slope, steering toward the center of the hill. The remaining attackers spread out around the vehicle, seven on the right flank keeping the defenders on the southern rim of the hill at bay. Four hugged its left flank, protecting it from suicide runners. Four more approached the foxholes along the northern rim, clearing each defender as they passed. Four more bombers attempted to take out the Hagglund, three from the northern rim and one from the south. None of them got closer than fifty feet to the vehicle.

"Run them over," yelled Cody from the back.

"Fuck off. They could be carrying C4."

Beast pressed forward. One hundred yards ahead of him,

he spotted the other side of the hill. They were almost home-free.

WE FAILED, THOUGHT Corporal Cynthia Waverly. *We only took out two of the Hagglunds. The third was about to crest the slope and outflank their primary defenses.*

Waverly and Private Turing had the easternmost foxhole on the hill. As Turing laid down suppressing fire, she grabbed her radio.

"This is Corporal Waverly. The enemy has breached the southern defenses with a Hagglund. I repeat. The enemy has breached—"

She did not notice the unexploded C4 device that landed at the bottom of her foxhole. She heard Turing scream, followed by an explosion. Their remains would never be found.

BEAST REACHED THE hill's eastern slope and headed down. The remaining eleven attackers followed close behind.

THIS IS CORPORAL Waverly. The enemy has breached the southern defenses with a Hagglund. I repeat. The enemy has breached—

Denning keyed the talk button on his radio. "Corporal Waverly, can you hear me?"

Silence.

Shit, they would never survive a three-pronged attack. He couldn't pull troops from the main defense line, especially with thousands of attackers bearing down on them. And the IDF personnel inside were heading off Caesar's force. That left only one option—his reserves.

Denning stepped inside the dome. "We have a breach of our defense. Unit Six, stay here. You're the last defense in case anyone gets inside. Units Seven and Eight, take up position to the west and south of the bay and don't let anyone through."

The units deployed as ordered. Once they were in place, Denning issued a second command.

"Close the bay doors."

THE ELEVATOR HAD almost reached the sub-basement level. Devon used his radio to call each IDF unit to assist them in stopping Caesar.

"That's taking too long," warned Maya. "Caesar will have overrun the place by the time we gather everyone."

"What do you suggest?"

Maya stepped over to the intercom that connected the entire facility.

Devon stopped her. "You'll cause a panic."

"Do you have a better idea?"

Devon moved aside. Maya pressed the talk button.

"Attention. Attention. We have a breach in the sub-basement of New Salem of approximately one hundred invaders. All IDF personnel, deploy there immediately. I repeat, all IDF personnel deploy to the lowest level of the New Salem sub-basement immediately. Everyone else, remain calm. We have the situation under control."

Maya and Devon jumped off when the elevator stopped, their weapons in the low-ready position, and headed for New Salem.

ONE OF THE attackers jumped Haskell as he climbed out of the foxhole, knocking him backward onto the ice. Haskell rolled, placing himself on top. He used his left hand to hold the attacker by the neck and reached for his M17 with the right.

"Die, motherfucker."

"You first." Haskell placed the barrel on the attacker's forehead and pulled the trigger.

All around him, his people engaged in hand-to-hand combat with the enemy. Though better trained, they were vastly outnumbered. Several of the attackers had already bypassed the forward line of defense and charged the second position. His people had to cross the Kill Zone, otherwise none of them would survive.

ARASAKI WATCHED THE forward line crumbled. He knew once the attackers reached their position, his troops would not hold out for long.

A young private, shivering from fear and his eyes wide with terror, stared at him. "What should we do, general?"

"Cover their retreat. And try not to shoot our people."

Arasaki aimed at an attacker charging them with a crowbar and pulled the trigger, killing the man instantly.

The private, bolstered by the former general, fired into the horde. Within seconds, the entire line gunned down the first elements of the advancing enemy.

BYRD PROVIDED COVER fire while Medugno climbed out of the foxhole. The two men had run only a few yards when a bullet struck the drill instructor in the right leg, blowing out his knee. Byrd collapsed, crying out in pain.

Medugno stopped. "Are you okay?"

"I'm hit. Get out of here while you can."

"Screw that." Medugno ran over and lifted Byrd, placing the drill instructor over his shoulders in a fireman's carry.

"Leave me, cadet."

"With all due respect, fuck you, sir."

Medugno rushed down the slope, using his Carbine to clear the attackers who had gotten in behind them.

CARVER SAW MEDUGNO carrying Byrd and heading for the main defense line. He ran over and joined them, bringing up their rear and shooting anyone who came too close.

BETTANY AND SANCHEZ had been cut off from the others, their position being one of the first overrun. Sanchez climbed out first and turned to cover Bettany when an attacker plunged a metal pitchfork into his face. One prong pierced his left eye, the second shattered several teeth and stuck in his mouth, and the third caught him in the throat. Sanchez fell backward, gurgling as he drowned in his blood.

Bettany emptied her Carbine into the attacker, tearing off everything above his chest. Someone to her right yelled. She spun around as two attackers lunged. The one carrying a baseball bat swung at her. She deflected the blow with her weapon and punched him in the face with the stock, knocking him unconscious.

The second attacker swung his axe, severing her right arm below the elbow. Shock overcame her as she stared at the limb oozing blood onto the floor of the foxhole. Bettany looked up as the attacker raised the axe above his head and brought it down, cleaving her head in half.

FEAR AND PANIC overcame Nori. He could neither shoot at the attackers or retreat, scared into inactivity. When a bullet struck down his comrade beside him, he broke down completely. Nori dropped to the bottom of the foxhole, pulled the body over him, and feigned death.

"WE DID IT." A sense of relief washed over Waters. The bay sat three hundred feet ahead of them. "I told you we'd—"

"Watch out," screamed Stephanie.

Only then did Waters realize his people aimed weapons at him. He swerved the Hagglund to the right and ducked to the side a moment before they fired. Bullets shattered the windshield and ricocheted inside the compartment. One tore through his shoulder. Most of the others ripped into Stephanie, leaving a mangled pile of flesh in the passenger's seat.

Thompson opened the rear door and stood. "Don't shoot. It's—"

A burst of gunfire blasted Thompson out of the Hagglund.

Waters kept driving, ignoring the blood spurting from his shoulder and the dizziness overcoming him. The bay stood less than a hundred feet away. He was almost home. Then he could see his wife and child.

Gunfire pummeled the Hagglund. Waters did not even notice. Another two rounds hit him in the chest and arm, though he barely realized it. He felt exhausted. Once he made it inside, he might take a nap before going to see… Who did he want to visit? Oh, right, his family. He wanted to be fully awake when—

Waters had maneuvered the Hagglund into the bay opening when a bullet caught him in the face, blowing him out of the driver's seat. He dropped to the compartment deck, releasing the controls. The vehicle stopped hallway into the bay. The closing doors crushed into its left flank, collapsing the Hagglund inward before grinding to a halt.

MEDUGNO RACED ACROSS the Kill Zone toward the main defense line, firing three-round bursts into anyone who got in his way. Carver followed behind, providing suppressing fire. Byrd felt useless being carried, so he withdrew his M17 and shot at the attackers in front of him. The gesture made him feel better but, being bounced around on the cadet's shoulder, only three bullets found their mark.

Around them, the remaining defenders dashed for safety.

Gunfire cut down a few. Others were tackled by the attackers and hacked to pieces with axes and bladed weapons. A dozen attackers had already reached the trench carved in front of the main defense line, only to be killed by the defenders. A layer of bodies and pools of blood formed at its base. Those not shooting reached over the ice wall and helped their people climb over the top.

Medugno's legs felt as if they would give out at any moment. If he didn't trip and fall, his heavy breathing and pounding chest would certainly kill him. Fifteen feet ahead of him stood a gap in the wall the attackers had not yet filled. Others reached over, urging him to hurry. Medugno took a deep breath and headed for the opening.

HASKELL AND ROBINSON followed close behind them and thirty feet to the right. They arrived at the wall. The hands of their comrades reached down to pull them to safety. A burst of gunfire from behind whizzed past Haskell, catching Robinson in the back and killing him instantly. The captain reached up and grabbed the outstretched hands when he heard a scream to his rear. He spun around.

The ten-year-old who had picked up the axe earlier charged him, the blade hovering over his head. Haskell raised his Carbine and fired a burst into the kid's right shoulder, tearing off his arm. The kid dropped onto the ice, holding the bloody stump and screaming.

Two sets of hands grabbed Haskell by the shoulders and pulled him over the wall to safety.

MEDUGNO REACHED THE wall and fell against it, exhausted. Several of the defenders lifted Byrd off his shoulders and dragged him across the wall. As they did, a stray round struck the drill instructor in the left ass cheek. It hurt like hell, but he would live.

"Hurry up," Medugno yelled to Carver as he cupped his hands to give his friend a foothold. In one quick motion, Carver placed his foot in Medugno's hands, launched himself onto the top of the ice wall, then spun around to help the others pull Medugno to safety.

Once on the other side, both men began firing at the approaching enemy.

Out of one hundred and fifty soldiers who had manned the first defensive position, only seventeen made it to the second line.

DENNING RAN TOWARD the Hagglund stuck in the bay.

"Open the doors and get that thing out of the way."

The bay door pulled aside ten feet and stopped. A lieutenant jumped into the driver's seat and attempted to move the Hagglund. The bay doors had disconnected the tracks and crushed the road wheels. It moved only a few feet and stopped, still blocking the entrance. A group of soldiers ran out, positioned themselves at the vehicle's rear, and started to push it inside.

More gunfire erupted from Units Seven and Eight.

PETERSON WATCHED THE attack from the top of the slope. For the first time since this madness began, he felt they might succeed.

The bulk of the attackers reached the trench. Stepping on the corpses of their comrades, they tried to vault over the ice wall, only to be gunned down, creating a barrier of the dead.

The second wave of attackers swarmed the wall, pushing against the others. Within minutes, a mass of five thousand people formed, fighting to climb over the top. Only a few hundred stayed back, primarily women and children standing north near the top of the slope to avoid being crushed or shot. This time the remaining twenty-five soldiers of Caesar's defense force didn't force them to march. The soldiers pushed through the crowd to join the fighting, pausing only to fire on the defenders.

So far, the enemy positions held, but victory was inevitable.

Charlotte and Maxine joined him.

"What are you doing here? I told you to stay in the Hagglund."

Charlotte wrapped her arm around her brother's. "We wanted to see how the battle is going."

Peterson patted her hand. "It's only a matter of time."

"WE DID IT." Beast could not believe their luck. Not only had they made it to the bay, but a damaged Hagglund sat in the opening, preventing the enemy from closing it.

Automatic weapons fire pelted his Hagglund, ricocheting harmlessly off the armor plating. Beast ignored it, concentrating on his target. He hoped to push the damaged Hagglund out of the way and get inside the elevator bay.

Beast rammed his Hagglund into the rear end of the broken-down vehicle. Rather than be pushed inside, the damaged Hagglund twisted to the left, blocking the entrance. Not a problem. He continued a few feet and pulled up alongside the portion of the bay doors that were closed. Defenders swarmed around him, firing wildly or trying to open the locked doors. Even better. His sacrifice would be worth a lot more now.

Removing the detonator from his pocket, he placed his thumb on the red button.

"For the glory of Caesar and the Empire."

Cody and Kevin repeated the call.

Beast pressed the button.

The two hundred pounds of C4 spread along the interior walls of the Hagglund exploded, ripping it apart. The defenders attempting to stop the vehicle and those pushing the damaged Hagglund out of the way were killed instantly. Denning among them. The explosion tore apart the damaged Hagglund, sending thousands of shards of shrapnel across the interior of the bay with devastating results. Half of Unit Six and most of those inside the bay were killed or incapacitated. The blast tore off the three closest sections of the sliding door and flung them onto the deck in mangled heaps. The next two panels were twisted and deformed, one of them hanging by the top sliders. They could not seal off the bay.

As catastrophic as the damage had been, the worst part had been the destruction of the switch that would initiate the Kill Zone.

CAESAR AND HIS men were five flights from the end of the stairwell when an explosion rocked the facility. Loose dust from the ceiling and walls rained down on them.

"What the fuck was that?" asked Crusher.

Caesar smiled. "It sounds like they breached the bay doors. Our people are about to invade."

A cheer went up from his men.

"Come on. Let's join them in the fight."

MAYA ENTERED THE lower sub-basement level of New Salem, the section used to maintain livestock. The animals cried and fidgeted in their pens, sensing the coming danger. She lifted her Carbine into the high-ready position and scanned the area as she walked, searching for Caesar. He hadn't arrived yet.

"Where's the stairwell?"

"Over there." Devon pointed to a door built into the wall five hundred yards away. "I don't see are any of the IDF personnel."

"Let's hope they get here before—"

A muffled explosion came from the topside, followed by a concussion wave flowing through the sub-basement a few seconds later. The livestock grew more agitated and tried to break out of their enclosures.

Maya focused on Devon. "What was that?"

"It sounds like they may have breached the elevator bay."

"Should we help them?"

Devon shook his head. "Two more bodies won't change anything. We need to stop Caesar."

ROMA LEFT HIS position in the elevator bay and checked on the damage caused by the explosion. A piece of shrapnel had grazed his forehead, slicing open the skin. Blood flowed down his face. He had been lucky, suffering a minor wound that would heal quickly. The blood proved nothing more than a nuisance.

The same could not be said for the others.

Corpses, limbs, and shattered machinery littered the floor. Those not seriously hurt tended to the wounded. Even worse, a gap of a hundred feet opened the bay to invasion. The general did not have enough troops to defend this position. That left him with only two options.

The general stepped over to a captain. "What's your name?"

The officer snapped to attention. "Captain DeFelice."

"Screw the formalities. Take the elevators to the sub-basement and disable the controls. If the attackers get in here, I don't want them to have a way to get to the lower levels."

"What about the wounded?" asked a sergeant caring for a woman with no arm who slowly bled out.

"Leave them. Our defenses could be breached at any second."

The sergeant looked at DeFelice for confirmation.

"You heard the General. Move."

As the soldiers carried out their orders, Roma searched the bay for the Kill Zone device, quickly giving up. Even if it survived the blast, he would never find it amongst the debris. Moving to the shattered doors, he stared out at the main defense line a quarter of a mile away and removed his radio from his belt.

"Colonel Philips, do you read me?"

ARASAKI GLANCED UP and down their positions. The situation had become desperate. So far, their position held but defending the wall from so many attackers had whittled down their numbers. It was only a matter of time before the enemy breached their defenses. Once that happened, and with no way to seal off the facility, defeat would be inevitable.

Beside him, the colonel's radio came to life. *Colonel Philips, do you read me?*

"I'm here."

This is General Roma. Activate the Kill Zone.

"Roger that." Philips placed down the radio.

Before he could do anything, one of Caesar's soldiers climbed onto the wall. Three defenders peppered him with gunfire, but not before the soldier emptied his Carbine into those beneath him. Philips' head exploded. His body fell back against the ice wall, blood streaming down the surface.

Philips, what the fuck is going on? Why haven't you activated the Kill Zone?

Arasaki picked up the radio. "The colonel is dead."

Is this Arasaki?

"Yes."

You do it.

The former general bowed his head. "I... I can't."

Listen, we have no way to defend the facility. If the enemy breaches your line, it's all over.

Arasaki scanned the line a second time. Off to his right, five attackers had made it over the wall and engaged in hand-to-hand combat with the defenders. Other defenders exploited the opportunity and crawled over. Over to his left, three defenders stood atop the wall, repelling the attackers, only to be pulled onto the other side. A lieutenant fifty feet away screamed at him do to it now before they were breached.

Arasaki picked up the detonator and pulled out the plunger. The red light in the corner went off and the green one came on.

"May my ancestors forgive me."

The general pushed down the plunger.

CHAPTER THIRTY-THREE

FIVE HUNDRED THERMITE charges spread out across the square mile of the Kill Zone detonated simultaneously, melting the ice to a depth of five feet. Those not killed outright in the blast fell into the water.

The remaining defenders crawled onto the wall to witness the carnage. Thousands of bodies floated on the surface. Those who survived the blast attempted to walk or swim to safety. In the frigid weather, the water began freezing immediately. Most, including all of Caesar's soldiers, quickly succumbed to hypothermia. Arasaki lost count of how many attackers trying to escape his troops gunned down, either venting their anger or ensuring few lived to fight again. Others attempting to wade to safety became trapped as the ice formed around them, ensuring a slow and painful death.

Those at the far end of the Kill Zone were luckier. They had less distance to cover to safety but still faced a five-foot wall of ice. None of them could climb out on their own. One by one, they dropped off the ledge. By hanging back during the attack, nearly a thousand stragglers remained safe on the western side of the zone. A few of the braver ones raced forward to help pull family and friends from an icy grave. They managed to rescue thirty-seven people from the water, the only ones to escape the Kill Zone. When the last ones were safe, the survivors retreated up the slope.

The lieutenant who had lambasted Arasaki a few moments earlier made his way to the former general.

"Sir, should we fire on them?"

He shook his head. "They pose no threat to us now."

Arasaki turned and scanned his position. Hundreds of dead and injured lay on the eastern side of the wall.

"Take the wounded inside so the medical staff can treat them, then come back and join us. And tell General Roma what happened."

"OH MY GOD." Maxine clasped a hand over her mouth.

Peterson agreed with the sentiment, too stunned to speak.

They had watched the thermite detonate and, when the smoke cleared, witnessed the death of the main assault force. Close to nine thousand people were killed instantly or condemned to a slow, horrible death. It would have sickened him if he had any emotion left in his soul. Almost thirty thousand people, an entire community, were wiped out in a week because of the grandeur of a madman.

And he had played a significant role in the massacre.

"What do we do now?" asked Charlotte.

What could they do? They had failed in taking USC7 and had no home to return to.

Charlotte squeezed his arm gently. "Brad?"

Peterson sighed. "We go back to the Hagglund and wait. Hopefully, Caesar will have better luck."

MAYA TOOK A position alongside the hog pen several yards from the door. Devon hid behind an electric trolley off to his left to transport carts of animals and meat around the complex. She flipped off the safety on her Carbine and set it on full-automatic mode. Checking her ammo pouch, she had eleven extra magazines for the Carbine and five for the M17.

The door leading to the emergency exit was sealed tight. Two thick metal cross beams, each secured with padlocks, kept anyone from casually using it. If Caesar hoped to break through, he would need C4.

Twenty-two members of the IDF filtered in from the other side of the sub-basement and made their way to Devon.

"I assume the enemy hasn't arrived yet," said a corporal who still had acne.

"They're expected any minute. Set up between Cadet Santos and me. Anything that comes through the door, shoot it."

"Yes, sir."

The IDF personnel deployed, laying prone and forming a semi-circle in front of the door.

Now they waited.

CAESAR REACHED THE bottom of the stairwell. Crusher raced forward and pushed on the door. "It's locked."

"Blow it."

Crusher removed three blocks of C4, attaching two to the hinges and one to the handle, then set the primer. Caesar ushered the rest of his men up to the second landing so the blast would shield them. When Crusher joined them, Caesar nodded. Crusher removed the detonator and set off the charges.

A roar filled the stairwell. The concussion knocked more dust from the ceiling and walls. When Caesar leaned over the railing, he saw that the metal door had been blasted away along with most of the jamb. Smoke and dust filled the area, providing cover.

Caesar turned to his soldiers.

"For the glory of the empire!"

"For the glory of Caesar and the empire!"

As one, the soldiers flowed down the stairs and into the sub-basement.

THE EXPLOSION CAUGHT Maya off guard even though she

expected it. She ducked as debris shot through the area. The door and metal bolts flew across the basement, coming to a rest in front of the line of IDF personnel. Thankfully, no one was injured.

Maya aimed her Carbine weapon at the door and wrapped her finger around the trigger.

The first eight soldiers through the opening died instantly in a hail of gunfire. Those behind them, anticipating resistance, burst through the door with guns blazing and fanned out to the right and left. A row of seven dumpsters, four on the left and three on the right, sat near the wall. Caesar's troops used them for cover.

Maya fired into the dumpster on the far right, her bullets impacting into the trash inside and leaving the attackers unscathed. Some of the IDF personnel did the same, most having the same results. Only one dumpster was empty, allowing the rounds to rip through the metal and tear apart the four attackers hiding behind it. The rest raised their Carbines above the lids and fired indiscriminately. Seven IDF personnel went down.

Several bullets blasted through the hog pen, killing three of the animals. The rest grew frantic, trying to escape. One round hit the metal post in front of Maya, ricocheting past her head, missing it by inches. She ignored the threat and kept on pumping bullets into the doorway.

Directing their fire against those inside the sub-basement meant diverting attention from the door, allowing more attackers to enter and spread out. Maya raced over to the other side of the hog pen to have a clear view of the dumpsters. Six of Caesar's men raced out from behind, attempting to outflank the IDF. Maya shot four of them, killing three. The wounded man clasped his abdomen and screamed. One of the attackers dragged him back to the dumpsters while the other provided covering fire. Maya fired her last two rounds, both catching the soldier in the chest.

Every time the IDF personnel paused to reload, more attackers rushed through the breach and spread out across the sub-basement. Maya realized they would be outflanked within minutes.

The attacker who had saved his friend peered around the corner of the dumpster, searching for Maya. She saw him first and fired five rounds. Two found their mark, splattering his head across the wall.

Twelve more IDF personnel filtered into the sub-basement and rushed to join the battle. Seven were killed or incapacitated in seconds, the survivors hiding behind the cattle pen. Maya needed to find a way to create a distraction that would allow the IDF personnel enough time to regroup. She had only one option, as stupid and desperate as it seemed.

Bounding over the railing of the pen, she crouched and made her way through the hogs toward the gate. Once certain no one had noticed her, she unlatched the gate and pushed it open. Over fifty terrified hogs bolted from the pen and dashed across the floor between the opposing forces.

Three of Caesar's soldiers charged the IDF, hoping to disrupt the unit, and wound up caught in the dash. The hogs ran them down. The animals' hoofs crushed them, their cries of agony overpowered by the terrified squealing of the hogs.

From behind the dumpsters and inside the doorway, Caesar's men used the opportunity to rain gunfire down on the defenders. None of the IDF personnel were hit, but a dozen hogs died in the crossfire, creating a panic. The hogs turned left and stampeded toward the opposite end of the sub-basement, which took them through the IDF, trampling to death three soldiers and critically wounding seven. Only those on either end of the line remained unscathed and had used those precious few seconds to reload and consolidate their positions.

DEVON KNEW HE could not reach the enemy through the

dumpsters, which left only one alternative.

Dropping prone, he peered under the trolley. The wheels on the dumpsters allowed a three-inch gap between the floor and their base. Devon saw boots through the gap. He lowered his Carbine and raked it back and forth. All seven soldiers fell to the floor, screaming in pain and clutching their wounds. Replacing the magazine with a full one, Devon fired under the dumpsters a second time, killing or incapacitating the attackers.

"FUCK THIS SHIT."

Caesar stood inside the stairwell, peering around the corner to watch the battle play out. His soldiers were trapped and could not move forward. The entire tide of battle would be decided in the next few seconds. They needed a diversion if they hoped to break the deadlock.

"Do we have any C4 left?"

Crusher stepped up and opened his shoulder bag. "Four more devices."

"Prepare two of them."

Crusher placed primer in two of the blocks then handed the detonator to Caesar. Both men leaned out and tossed the explosives. One landed near the trolley and the other in front of the IDF personnel. Both men ducked behind the jamb. Caesar pressed the button.

The device near the trolley pummeled the vehicle with shrapnel, shredding the IDF officer firing on the enemy. The blast spared Devon because he had taken cover behind the tires as he switched out magazines. The explosion near the IDF personnel decimated the remainder of the line. Nine died, three bleeding out from their injuries, and six were wounded. The rest were shocked by the concussion. Taking advantage of the situation, Caesar's remaining soldiers flowed out of the stairwell and emerged from behind the dumpsters, charging the defenders and gunning down anyone in sight.

DEVON MOVED TO the end of the trolley. He spotted six soldiers racing across the floor toward his position. None made it. Devon ducked behind the trolley to reload. Someone ran up to his right.

"Cover me while I—" He looked up. One of Caesar's soldiers hovered over him. Devon went for his sidearm. Before he could reach it, the soldier slammed the stock of his Carbine into Devon's face, knocking him out.

MAYA TOOK THE opportunity created by the twin explosions. She switched out her magazine with a full one and rushed the dumpsters. Three soldiers emerged, stunned to see her. Before they could aim their weapons, Maya gunned them down.

She circled behind the dumpster. Seven soldiers were preparing to charge the facility. Maya had caught them off guard and emptied her Carbine into them. Four went down. The other three were wounded. Maya slid her M17 from its holster and, while walking past them, double-tapped each in the face.

Two more soldiers rushed out of the door as she approached. Maya fired four more rounds. Three ripped open the chest of the nearest and wounded the other in the arm. She shot him in the back of her head. The slide on her pistol locked open.

As Maya replaced the empty magazine, Crusher came through the doorway, stepped up to her, and punched her in the abdomen. The air rushed out of her lungs. She doubled over in pain. The soldier grabbed Maya by the hair, lifted her, and slammed her face against the wall. A bolt of pain shot from her cheek through her head. For a moment, her vision blurred. Crusher yanked Maya to one side. A tall man with a grim expression stood in front of her. Only then did Maya realize the gunfire had ceased.

"You're a feisty little one." The tall man turned to the soldier. "Bring her."

"Yes, Caesar." Clutching her tight by the hair, Crusher pulled her around the dumpsters.

Only four of her people had survived the attack, including Devon, who now stood in front of the trolley. Just under twenty of Caesar's soldiers remained, forming a semi-circle around the prisoners. More than enough to take the facility. They had failed.

Crusher shoved Maya beside Devon.

"Are you okay?" he asked.

Maya nodded.

"What should we do with them?" asked Abbott.

Caesar withdrew his M17 and walked down the line, putting bullets in the forehead of the three IDF personnel. He paused when he reached Maya, lowering his weapon.

"You might be of use. On your knees and show deference to your new leader."

Maya sneered. "I'd rather die on my feet than live on my knees."

"Doesn't matter to me." Caesar raised the M17 and aimed at her head.

Maya closed her eyes.

She heard the bullet fired and flinched. Warm blood ran down her face, but it did not belong to her. She opened her eyes.

Devon stood in front of Maya. He had stepped in front of her and taken the bullet. The gore had come from him. The back of Devon's head was missing. His body teetered for a moment, then collapsed onto the floor.

"Fuck you!" Maya screamed so loud spittle flew from her lips.

Caesar placed the M17 against her forehead. "I don't have time for—"

A crowbar came sailing from somewhere to her right. It slammed into Crusher's head. He dropped his weapon. A chunk of cement caught Abbott, fracturing his skull.

Several hundred citizens of USC7 rushed Caesar's soldiers. Each carried whatever they could find as weapons—axes, crowbars, chunks of cement, pieces of pipe, meat cleavers. Some of the soldiers fired back, but there were too many citizens to stop. They rushed the attackers, beating them into a bloody pulp. Crusher fought back, snapping the neck of one of the citizens. Five citizens knocked him to the ground, beating him with pipes and crowbars until a sixth shattered Crusher's head with a block of cement.

Several of Caesar's men broke and ran, only to be chased down and butchered.

Maya grabbed Caesar's wrist in her left hand and pushed his arm out of the way. The M17 fired, the bullet missing her head by inches. She wrapped her right hand around the pistol and twisted, disarming Caesar. Maya turned the weapon on him.

Caesar pushed Maya's right hand away with his left and rammed the palm of his right hand into her nose. She felt the bone shatter. Blood poured over her mouth and chin. The momentary shock caused her to drop the pistol. Caesar kicked the M17 across the floor and moved behind Maya in the brief second that the blow stunned her. He wrapped his left arm around her throat and closed it against her larynx, using his other to tighten his grip, closing off her oxygen supply.

Panic set in as she gasped for breath. Maya needed to break the hold. Remembering what Byrd had taught her, she slammed her head back against Caesar's face as hard as she could. The movement allowed Caesar to clasp his arm tighter around her neck. Maya felt her brain becoming foggy from lack of oxygen. This had better work.

The first blow had no effect. Maya slammed her head back again. The second blow broke Caesar's nose. Maya felt blood running down the back of her head. Summoning what little energy she had left, Maya whipped her head back a third time. A loud crack sounded, followed by Caesar crying out. His grip loosened. Maya shifted her body to the left, breaking his chokehold, and rammed her right elbow into Caesar's face. A louder crack sounded and he released his grip. Maya fell on her hands and knees, gasping for air.

Caesar stepped back and spit. Three teeth and a pool of blood landed on the floor. "You cunt!"

All Maya had the energy to do was flip him her middle finger.

Caesar raced forward and kicked out with his right leg. Maya caught the knee in her right hand, lessening the blow, and wrapped her left arm around the leg. She applied downward pressure, hoping to shatter the kneecap. Caesar fell back and shifted his body to the right, swinging his left leg in an arch that caught Maya on the back of her head. She released Caesar's leg and fell to the floor, rolling onto her back, dazed. She expected him to go for the M17 and execute her.

Instead, Caesar stepped up, raised his right leg over her head, and kicked down. Maya blocked the blow with her hands. Clutching his foot, she spun her body to the left, kicking the other leg out from under him. Caesar collapsed onto the floor, landing on his shoulder. Maya released his leg and crawled across the cement after him. He stopped her with a kick to the abdomen that sent a crippling wave of pain through her body.

Rather than continue the fight, Caesar scrambled to his feet and ran for the emergency stairwell.

THE EUPHORIA OF victory had given way to the panic of saving his life. Caesar limped away from the psychotic bitch. He needed to get out of there before that angry mob turned on him.

Blood covered the cement around the battlefield, making it difficult to walk without slipping. Once clear of the melee, he picked up a stray Carbine laying on the ground and removed an ammunition pouch from one his shoulders, then headed for the door where the bag with the last two C4 devices lay. That should be more than enough to cover his retreat.

As he entered the doorway, he paused long enough to survey the scene one last time. To his surprise, the crazed bitch he had severely beaten followed him.

Fuck her.

Caesar raised the Carbine and fired.

MAYA STRUGGLED TO get up, trying to ignore the pain. Through her blurred vision, she saw Caesar running for the stairwell. The fucking coward was trying to save himself. She struggled to get up, trying to ignore the pain. For a moment, she considered letting him go, then her eyes fell on Devon, his face toward her, the lifeless eyes meeting her own. The memory of him giving his life to save hers rushed her thoughts. Caesar had taken the most important person in her life. No way would she left that motherfucker quietly freeze to death. He deserved to suffer.

Climbing to her feet, Maya staggered over to an abandoned Carbine, picked it up, and limped after Caesar.

Caesar had entered the doorway leading to the emergency stairwell. He turned and spotted her, raised his weapon, and fired.

Maya dived to the floor and rolled against the corpse of one of Caesar's soldiers. Pain shot through her body, numbing her senses. She heard bullets thudding into flesh, hoping none of them struck her. None did. When the firing stopped, she raised her head. Caesar had disappeared up the stairs.

Struggling to her feet, Maya limped across the sub-basement and paused at the jamb. She peered around the corner, expecting an ambush. Caesar's footsteps echoed off the stairs above her. She ejected the magazine and checked. It contained bullets, though she had no idea how many. Finding another weapon would take too long. She inserted the magazine back into the Carbine, cocked a round into the chamber, and set off after Caesar.

CAESAR REACHED THE twentieth landing, huffing for breath, when he heard footsteps below him. That cunt wouldn't give up. This time he would stop her for good.

Continuing to climb, Caesar removed one of the blocks of C4 from the bag, set the primer, and stopped before the next landing. He leaned over the rail. When she appeared three flights below, Peterson tossed the block at her. Running up to the landing where he would be shielded from the blast, he detonated the C4.

A cloud of smoke and dust blew up through the central opening. Cracks formed in the stairs and along the wall, and dust shook loose from the walls. Once the noise settled, he listened. No more footsteps. Good.

Caesar continued to the ice tunnel.

THE BLOCK OF C4 landed on the stairs three feet in front of Maya and bounced down the steps. She hugged the wall and ran as fast as she could to avoid the blast, making it as far as the next landing when the explosive ignited.

Maya fell flat as chunks of concrete and metal blasted up the central opening. Smoke and dust rolled over her, and she felt the stairs beneath her give way. Reaching out with her left hand, Maya desperately grabbed for anything to stop her fall, her hand clutching the guardrail. She felt her legs dangling, but at least she no longer fell. Shouldering the Carbine, she grabbed the railing with her right hand and pulled herself up. Excruciating pain wracked her body, but she ignored it. She hoped the section of stairs beneath her would not collapse under her weight.

Her right knee bumped into jagged concrete. Lifting her leg, Maya braced it on the broken step and pulled with her arms. A few seconds later, her left leg landed on the step. She carefully made her way to the landing and stopped. The blast tore away one landing and two sections of the stairwell. If it had gone off a second earlier, she would be laying among the debris covering the floor below.

Taking a moment to catch her breath, Maya stood and set off after Caesar.

CAESAR PAUSED ON the fortieth landing to rest. He heard footsteps several landings beneath him. Fuck, that bitch must have nine lives like a cat. Opening the bag, he removed the last block of C4 and set the primer. He planned on using it to seal the ice tunnel once he made his escape. Hopefully, he wouldn't have to use it early.

MAYA FORCED HERSELF to keep going. Her legs ached from the climb and her chest throbbed. She was already far behind Caesar because of her wounds and getting trapped on the collapsed stairs. If she stopped to rest, the bastard would escape. She couldn't allow that.

CAESAR REACHED THE final landing in front of the ice tunnel. He leaned against the wall to catch his breath.

He had made it. Fuck the others. They failed because they were weak. He had survived because he was strong. He deserved to live. Once out of this hell hole, he would find Peterson, then he and the girls would seek out another facility to settle down in, one that he could eventually take over as—

"Don't move or you're dead."

Caesar's gaze focused on the landing below. The bitch had

caught up with him. She had her Carbine trained on him and laboriously climbed the steps one at a time, leaning her right shoulder against the wall. The bitch looked like shit from the beating he had given her but, with the weapon trained on him, she could still get a drop on him if he went for his weapon.

Which left only one option.

Caesar bolted down the ice tunnel.

MAYA FIRED A three-round burst when Caesar headed for the tunnel. All three bullets missed.

"Shit."

Maya climbed the last few steps and centered herself at the end of the ice tunnel. Caesar stood twenty-five feet away facing her, one hand holding the block of C4 over his head and the other clasping the detonator, his finger on the button.

"Looks like we have ourselves a stalemate." Caesar had a deranged smile on his face. "If you shoot me, I set off the explosives, and you're close enough to die in the blast."

"I don't care."

"Bullshit, otherwise you would have shot me by now. Drop your weapon over the railing or we both die."

Maya hesitated.

"Now!"

Maya removed her finger from the trigger, held the Carbine by its barrel, dangled the weapon over the central opening, and released it.

"Good girl." Caesar backed down the tunnel, his gaze fixed on Maya. "You stay right where you are and we'll both live to see another day."

Not if I have anything to say about it, thought Maya.

She waited until Caesar backed another fifty feet down the tunnel then withdrew the M17 from its holster. She did not aim for Caesar but the C4 in his hand. The third round struck its target, igniting the block. The explosion ripped Caesar apart and weakened the tunnels' structure. It collapsed, burying Caesar's remains under a ton of ice.

The concussion flowed out of the tunnel and slammed into Maya, propelling her against the guardrail. She felt her shoulder blades crack against the metal then slid to the landing, watching as the son of bitch receive the end he deserved.

As smoke and ice crystals flowed around her, Maya slipped away.

NORI PUSHED THE corpse off him and crouched, slowly peering over the rim of his foxhole. Carnage spread out around him. Thousands of corpses littered the battlefield, most belonging to the enemy, but too many were his fellow soldiers—men and women who dared to face overwhelming odds and died for their conviction.

He fell back into the foxhole and cried. Despair filled his soul. Nori had proven himself to be a coward, had hidden while his friends fought and died. Not only had he brought shame upon himself, he had also betrayed the EDF and brought disgrace to his family. Wiping away the tears, he summoned the courage to make the only honorable choice.

Climbing out of the foxhole and checking to make sure nobody saw him, Nori set off into the tundra. Everyone would believe he had died in battle rather than slink off to let the frozen world take him.

"CAESAR, ARE YOU there?" Peterson waited several seconds for a reply. None came.

"Caesar, do you hear me?" Still nothing.

"Can anyone hear me?"

Peterson turned off the radio and tossed it on the dashboard. He placed his arms on top of the steering wheel and placed his chin on his wrists, staring blankly across the tundra as he figured out the next course of action.

He did not have a lot of choices.

Almost everyone from New Empire had died—Caesar, the defense forces, the fighting units, and nearly every citizen. The few thousand that held back from the attack and survived the thermite explosion had rescued what few survivors remained and then headed into the tundra. Peterson had no idea where they were going. There was nowhere to go. He assumed they headed off to die on their own terms.

He faced the same option.

They had a weeks' worth of rations for five people. If they rationed the food, they could stretch those supplies to a month. He had heard rumors of other facilities still functioning down south, one in New Jersey, one near Washington D.C., and a third somewhere in the south. Maybe these rumors would turn out to be true.

Peterson sat up in his seat, started the engine, and drove off to the south.

"Where are we going?" asked Charlotte.

"To start a new life for ourselves."

CHAPTER THIRTY-FOUR

Two days later

BYRD FOUND IT hard to get comfortable in his hospital bed. If he lay on his left side to favor his wounded leg, his ass hurt. When he switched positions to take the pressure off his behind, his leg throbbed. He refused to ask for morphine, knowing the seriously wounded needed it more.

"Good morning, sir."

Byrd rolled over to face the door, making a concerted effort not to grunt or show how much pain he suffered. Medugno and Carver stood in his room, the latter putting his weight on a cane, his right leg bandaged.

"It's good to see you two made it through okay. How are the other cadets?"

Both men stared at each other. Carver finally answered. "Except for Maya, we're the only ones who survived."

Byrd closed his eyes and fought back the tears.

Medugno changed the topic. "How are you doing?"

"The leg wound is pretty bad. My knee is gone. The doctors said they can replace it, but I'll walk with a limp. I guess my days of being a pain in the ass to cadets is over."

"I doubt that, sir." Carver put on a pleasant demeanor. "We lost most of the defense force in the battle. I'm sure command will want you to train their replacements."

"I hope you're right, son."

"The nurse said you received two wounds. Where's the other one?"

"I got shot in the buttocks." Neither cadet got Byrd's refer-

197

ence to that old Tom Hanks movie. God, he was getting old.

Medugno tried to break the awkward moment. "Don't expect me to kiss it and make it feel better."

"That's enough out of you, corporal."

Medugno snapped to attention. "I'm sorry, sir. I meant no…. Did you call me corporal?"

Byrd smiled, something he rarely did around the cadets. "I told General Roma how you saved my life and recommended you both for commendations and that you skip a rank. The general approved. Congratulations."

"Thank you, sir," both men responded simultaneously, stunned yet honored.

"I don't know how to repay you," said Medugno.

"There's no need to repay me. You earned it. I only hope that when General Roma asks you to help train the new cadets, you'll both agree."

"We will, sir," responded Carver.

"It'll be an honor." Medugno paused. "Who'll be training us?"

Byrd grinned.

Medugno stood tall. "I'm looking forward to it."

Byrd's butt wound hurt like hell lying on it for so long. He was grateful when one of the nurses stepped into the room and crossed her arms across her chest.

"You two have to go now. The sergeant needs to rest."

Both men headed for the door.

"Gentlemen," said Byrd.

They turned to him. Byrd gave them a crisp salute. Medugno and Carver snapped to attention, returned the salute, and left.

Byrd settled back in bed, this time favoring his ass wound. The death of so many good men and women who gave their lives defending the facility weighed heavily on him.

At least the future would be in good hands.

Four days later

MAYA RODE THE one functioning elevator topside to check on the recovery efforts.

After the blast that had killed Caesar, she had passed out from pain and exhaustion, only coming to three hours later when a rescue party discovered her unconscious by the ice tunnel. They took her to med bay where the doctors informed her she had suffered three broken ribs, a fractured shoulder blade, a broken nose, a mild concussion, and several severe bruises, most of it from the fistfight in the sub-basement. The doctors wrapped her wounds and gave her pain killers to ease her recovery. The doctors advised her to remain in bed for a week, but Maya checked herself out after twenty-four hours of bed rest. She had too much to do.

General Roma had asked her to take over Devon's role as head of the intelligence unit. At first, she declined, saying she did not have the qualifications. The general pointed out that she had been the one to recommend the trench in front of the main defense line and had figured out what Caesar had planned. Without her, they would all be living under Caesar's rule. Maya reluctantly agreed.

The following six days had been a whirlwind of activity. The day after the battle, Governor Mangerian resigned her position as head of the government and passed the mantle to Riviera, her opponent in the rigged election. Ostensibly, she claimed she wanted a new government to lead the reconstruction of USC7. Maya knew that was only partially correct. The governor had an emotional breakdown between the stealing of the election, the damage to the facility, and the number of lives lost on both sides. Mangerian had hoped to retire from politics. To her chagrin, Riviera asked her to be his advisor during the transition.

Rivera's first decision after assuming the governorship had been a humanitarian one. On the day after the battle, three hundred and sixty-seven survivors showed up at the bay seeking asylum. They were among those who had retreated after Caesar's defeat and had chosen to live rather than allow the elements to kill them. Riviera agreed under the condition that they are prisoners for three years. Citizens from Ring D who had volunteered to replace the defense force personnel lost in combat were given new quarters in Ring C, and the prisoners occupied their old spaces. The children and elderly would work in Ring E. Those more capable would clear the battlefields and repair the damage to the facility. If they worked hard and did not cause trouble, they would be granted full citizen status after their term of imprisonment. Everyone readily agreed. Even the worse conditions in USC7 were far better than what they had gone through in New Empire.

The elevator reached the upper bay and stopped. Work crews had piled the wreckage from the explosion in the center of the floor where engineers sorted through it to find anything salvageable. Work crews made of prisoners repaired the damaged bay doors. Six of the panels were irreparable, so prison crews removed panels from the bay door sealed off by snow and ice and used them.

Maya zipped up her coat, pulled the hood over her head, and donned her sunglasses. The tight-fitting clothing aggravated the pain in her chest and shoulders, and the sunglasses made her nose ache. Maya ignored the discomfort and exited. Light snow fell. Good. That would at least cover the blood frozen across the area.

She made her way to the main defense line where three tables had been set up. One contained weapons used by the attackers, all melee type since the enemy's Carbines and pistols had been lost in the Kill Zone. A pile of cold-weather clothes and boots, the outfits removed from both sides who had died in battle, sat on the second table, overflowing onto the ground. The extra uniforms would allow more people access to Above Earth. Three intelligence officers stood around the third table, thumbing through diaries, letters, maps, and other items that could provide valuable information. Her analysts would have a field day rummaging through this pile.

"Did you find anything interesting?"

The three soldiers came to attention. A corporal responded with, "No, ma'am."

"Stop the saluting and the 'ma'am' shit, please."

"Yes, ma… sir."

"Call me Maya."

"As you say, ma'am."

Maya sighed mentally. "What do you have?"

"From a cursory glance, nothing of intel value. Most of this stuff describes life inside New Empire. It was a fuck…. sorry, a nightmare. Once the analysts look over the paperwork, we'll pass it to the historical branch."

"Good call."

"Maya." Haskell stood on the ice wall overlooking the trench, waving for her to join him.

When Maya reached the top, she got her first look at the Kill Zone. Snow fell across the slope, but not enough to hide the thousands of bodies trapped under the ice. Prison works crews used chainsaws to remove any limbs sticking up from the surface. A week ago, the sight would have made her vomit. Now she took it in stride.

Maya nodded her head toward the Kill Zone. "What are you going to do about them?"

"Nothing. It's too much trouble to dig them out. We're piling up the enemy dead at the base of the ice cliff. Then we're going to level the ice wall and fill in the trench. In a few weeks, everything will be covered in snow and ice. Nobody will know a battle took place here."

"We will," Maya mumbled. "What about our people?"

"Governor Riviera wants to cremate our people and place the ashes in urns. He plans on setting up a memorial hall for them. It's the least we can do."

Maya thought for a moment. "I heard there's a trail of dead bodies leading from New Empire."

Haskell frowned. "We have only one Hagglund left—the one Caesar used. We sent it out to make sure Caesar had not been preparing a secondary strike. All they found were corpses stretching for five miles. We're going to leave them. It's good enough for them."

"Once we clear up things here, we'll need to remove them. They're a trail marker for any others out there."

Haskell's eyes widened. "Do you think that's a possibility?"

"Do you want to take the chance?"

"Good point."

Maya glanced at her watch. "I have to go."

"Okay. We'll let you know if we find anything of intel value."

"Thanks."

Maya took one last look at the Kill Zone before going back inside, shaking her head.

✧　✧　✧

MAYA SAT IN the front row seat of the auditorium, waiting for the memorial service to begin. They were here to pay tribute to the over nine hundred men and women of the EDF and IDF who died in battle. Despite the odds, they had repelled the invasion and eliminated any future threat from New Empire, but at staggering losses. In addition to their own, patrols counted over eleven thousand attackers killed. Most of the survivors had retreated into the tundra.

Maya turned in her chair to view the audience. All defense force personnel were busy with other assignments. Families and friends of the deceased filled the hall. The impact of the losses struck her when she saw that the hall had exceeded capacity, with people standing against the wall five deep. She had been allowed to attend because of her relationship with Devon.

A hand rose from the crowd, and her father waved. Maya waved back, and Anthony beamed. Her mother Esther sat beside him, crying from relief because Maya was still alive and proud of her daughter saving the facility. Even her brother seemed proud. Carlos smiled at her and nodded.

Riviera, Mangerian, General Roma, and the eight mayors entered the hall and took their places on the podium. Photos of the nine hundred and twenty-three defense personnel and citizens who had died adorned the wall. They filled the space. Maya scanned the images, finding Devon's picture near the center. She realized now that he had loved her as much, if not more than she had loved him. He had given his life to save her. Eventually, the grief would lessen, and the daily struggle to keep going would become easier, but she would never get over losing Devon and would never stop loving him.

Riviera stepped up to the microphone. "Ladies and gentlemen, it's with a heavy heart that I address you this morning. Not since the first months of the Great Freeze have we bore witness to a tragedy such as this. Too many citizens—family, loved ones, and friends—gave their lives to defend USC7. Their sacrifice, though heavy, was not in vain. By the grace of God and their courage, we survived the assault, and our democracy continues to thrive. We are here today to both honor their memory and their contribution."

Maya tuned out the rest of the ceremony, thinking about Devon and the life they could have had together.

A Thank You to My Readers

In addition to working for the CIA and being a step-dad, writing has been one of the most fulfilling things I've done with my life. The best part is having fans who read my books, enjoy them, and want more. I'm incredibly fortunate and grateful I have such a loyal fanbase. You keep reading, and I'll keep writing.

If you enjoyed *Frozen World*, please post a review on Amazon and Goodreads. Reviews are what drive the algorithms that get a writer's books more exposure. It doesn't have to be lengthy—just a rating and a sentence or two about why you liked or disliked it. To be successful in this genre, I need your support.

Thank you all in advance.

Acknowledgments

The fun part of my job is writing. The difficult part is getting my books published. It's a complicated process involving many people, all of whom deserve to be recognized.

This is my first novel that does not involve zombies, vampires, demons, or other creatures of the night. I was nervous at first stepping outside my comfort zone, but I became engrossed in this project once I did. I want to thank my social media manager for pushing me to write *Frozen World*, as well as my many writer friends who understood my trepidation and offered support.

Many thanks to all the veterans who sent me their boot camp stories. I used some of them. However, most of the run-ins between the cadets and Byrd came from one person's personal experiences—my father. In addition to raising his two children, his proudest moments were when he served in the Marine Corps in the late 1950s. He constantly regaled me with his basic training escapades when I was little. As a tribute to him, many of those made their way in the boot camp scenes.

Many thanks also go out to my beta readers. Most of whom have been with me from book one. They point out grammatical/spelling errors and inconsistencies and offer their opinion on whether they like the story. I would be lost without them. With regards to *Frozen World*, Doc Fried proved a Godsend. He pointed out numerous plot flaws and errors that would have significantly detracted from the story. This book is a much better read because of it.

Warren Design created the cover art for *Frozen World*, as

they have for several other of my books. Their work perfectly fits the mood of this book. I'm looking forward to working with them in the future.

Finally, a major debt of thanks goes to my family, human and furry. Working from home allows me to set my hours, though it's rare if I work less than ten hours a day. The pets are always there as my muses and distractions. Walther and Bella sit with me on my porch while I write during the day (except in the freezing weather when they abandon me for a warm bed) and, at night when I'm in my study editing and managing social media, my cats Archer and Michonne stand in front of my desktop, Michonne because she wants to be petted and Archer to meow because he ran of treats or because he can see the bottom of his food dish. My family never complains (I think they're glad to get rid of me). I couldn't do this without their love, patience, and support.

About the Author

Scott M. Baker was born and raised in Everett, Massachusetts and spent twenty-three years in northern Virginia working for the Central Intelligence Agency and traveling through Europe, Asia, and the Middle East. Scott is now retired and lives outside of Concord, New Hampshire, with his wife and fellow writer Alison Beightol, his stepdaughter, two rambunctious Boxers, and two cats who treat him as their human servant. He is currently writing the *Nurse Alissa vs. the Zombies* saga, his latest zombie apocalypse series, and his paranormal series. Previous works include the *Shattered World* series, his five-book young adult post-apocalypse thriller about a group of adventurers attempting to close interdimensional portals from Hell; *The Vampire Hunters* trilogy, about humans fighting the undead in Washington D.C.; *Rotter World*, *Rotter Nation*, and *Rotter Apocalypse*, his first post-apocalyptic zombie saga; *Yeitso*, his homage to the giant monster movies of the 1950s that he loved watching as a kid; as well as several zombie-themed novellas and anthologies.

Please check out Scott's social media accounts for the latest information on future books, upcoming events, and other fun stuff.

Facebook: facebook.com/groups/397749347486177
Twitter: twitter.com/vampire_hunters
Instagram: instagram.com/scottmbakerwriter
Blog: scottmbakerauthor.blogspot.com